The Wonder of Charlie Anne

The Wonder of Charlie Anne

KIMBERLY NEWTON FUSCO

Alfred A. Knopf
New York

THIS IS A BORZOI BOOK PUBLISHED BY ALFRED A. KNOPF

Visit us on the Web! www.randomhouse.com/kids

Educators and librarians, for a variety of teaching tools, visit us at www.randomhouse.com/teachers

Library of Congress Cataloging-in-Publication Data
Fusco, Kimberly Newton.
The wonder of Charlie Anne / Kimberly Newton Fusco. — 1st ed.
p. cm.
Summary: In a 1930s Massachusetts town torn by the Depression and other hardships, as well as racial tension, Charlie Anne and Phoebe, the black girl who moves next to the farm next door, form a friendship that begins to transform their community.
ISBN 978-0-375-86104-8 (trade) — ISBN 978-0-375-96104-5 (lib. bdg.) — ISBN 978-0-375-89555-5 (e-book)
[1. Race relations—Fiction. 2. Farm life—Massachusetts—Fiction. 3. Depressions—1929— Fiction. 4. Friendship—Fiction. 5. African Americans—Fiction. 6. Family life— Massachusetts—Fiction. 7. Massachusetts—History—20th century—Fiction.] I. Title.
PZ7.F96666Won 2010
[Fic]—dc22
2009038831

The text of this book is set in 13-point Goudy.

Printed in the United States of America
August 2010
10 9 8 7 6 5 4 3 2 1

First Edition

For my children—
Daniel, Matthew, Kate and Laura

I

Go do this, the new mama tells me, and I do it, just because.

Look in that cupboard because maybe there's something in there, maybe a mouse. Or maybe not, maybe it's just a shadow from that old pee pot in there, the new mama isn't sure. But I better do it, just because.

I know just because. Just because means I am a girl, and a girl needs to know about things, like keeping whites from colors in the washbucket and why you sweep before you mop, and about keeping your legs crossed all the time and how to rub a skinny little chest with Vicks while you're wiping a nose. Two things at once, that's what you do. Keep your cow from running in the road at the same time you're trying to get all these peas shelled for supper. And do be quiet while the new mama talks, on and on.

"You better listen when I'm talking because I'm not going to say it twice, Charlie Anne. Put on some beans, and why don't you mix up some biscuits, nice and high like your papa likes them, and how come these underpants aren't ironed right? They're rough as shingles. Don't you listen to a thing I say?"

I turn and look as far as I can see. *No, ma'am.* The new buttercups bloomed this morning. Can't you hear them? They are singing, and I can hear their tiny voices calling out to me, and the bees are buzzing inside that apple tree so loud I can hardly think about the laundry that still needs hanging.

But the loudest voice is the river that races right across our fields. It says, Hurry, Charlie Anne, hurry. It says it all the time.

This is how we got so many babies around here.

One morning when I am small I walk out to check on our cow, Anna May, and nestled up against her is a new little calf with eyes as dark as a full jar of molasses. I pull my milk stool over and sit and watch Anna May and how happy she is nuzzling her first baby calf and I get to thinking about how I would like to have little babies in the house for me to play with so I will have more than just Thomas, who is too old, and Ivy, who tells on me all the time. So I pray to the angels that they will bring my mama a baby. I pray awfully hard because Anna May's calf is so gosh darn cute and he just about splits my heart like an old melon and before I know it we have two babies in our house, split, splat. First Peter and then before I know it another baby, Birdie, who will not eat anything but biscuits, blackberry jam and lemon drops. Mama gets all tired and

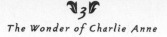

worn out from her new babies and she gets a cross look when I ask if she wants to go to our favorite spot by the river.

My prayers keep on strong as rock because, before I know it, there's another baby, the one who takes Mama straight to heaven as soon as she is born. I stop praying to the angels after that. Prayers are powerful things.

After lunch I stomp outside because the new mama says I have to go get all the laundry I just hung up. It is going to rain and I have to take it all down and hang it in the barn. I don't want to take down everything I already hung up. The sun will dry it all over again tomorrow, and besides, I want to go to the river, I tell her. I have already been doing chores since I woke up. The new mama tells me to get the laundry, or else.

The new mama is the cousin Mirabel from two towns over. Papa did not ask her, she just showed up one day after the funeral with her suitcases, all strapped up tight, and her shoes that snap when she walks. After Mama left us, Papa walked around like a horse kicked him in the belly, so he did not say much when Mirabel told Peter and Birdie to move up to the attic with Ivy and me. Since Thomas was already fifteen, he could sleep in the barn. I asked why couldn't I do that. Why couldn't I sleep with Anna May and our chickens, Minnie and Olympia and Bea, instead of Peter, who still wets the bed. Mirabel told me right then and there that I was going to learn some manners, or else. None of us like Mirabel, me especially. I think she has her eyes on Papa in a bad way.

I stomp outside.

Actually, I am afraid of me dying from all my chores. I reach up and check my heart. It is all skittering and I sit down on the clothes basket and let it rest. Mirabel tells me not to worry, I am strong as an ox. I hear the screen door bang, and before I know it, she is out on the porch with her hands on her hips yelling for me to help her with the lunch. I jump up and start pulling down all the laundry I already hung up, and when I do, I hear the river calling me again: Hurry, Charlie Anne, hurry.

I believe it wants to be listened to.

For a long time, I think it is the "Charlie Anne River." My mama told me it was true, it was the Charlie Anne River even if no one else knew that.

Everything has a song, a kindness, if you just take the time to listen, she told me one night when she was pushing me on my swing in the old elm tree by the barn. We were listening to the owls and the peepers and watching the bats flit across the sky right in front of us. That was back when she used to call me her singing butterfly. "Lots of people don't know how to listen, Charlie Anne. But when you do, you know things that other people don't." After that I started putting my ear to the turnips growing in the garden, to the barn door, even to Anna May, and listening for their songs.

That is how I know the river likes my name very much. I hear it singing Charlie Anne, Charlie Anne when I am sitting high on the ridge, watching it rush over the rocks and out of my sight. It is a name the wind likes, too. I hear it singing my name in the afternoon when it is sending a quiet little breeze big enough to cool me down after I have been carrying wood for our wood box all morning. There is a kindness to the river and the wind and to lots of other things, if you only take the time to listen, I tell Mirabel. She gets that cross look on her face when I say that, that the trees are singing and the clothesline is tired from its clothes from yesterday and it doesn't want me to hang up that old rug.

Back before Peter and Birdie came along, back before the last baby, who took Mama away forever, I used to pretend that I was the river. Sometimes I was the summer river, moving all slow and lazy, and singing to the blueberries that stretched almost halfway to the other side, and offering up drinks to the little fawns that still had spots on them. Now when Mirabel yells what is taking so long with the laundry, I am the spring river, big and fast and in an awful hurry to get away from here.

Wait, I tell the river. Wait for me. But it doesn't wait. It rushes faster, off to someplace else, and I watch it go.

2

Papa wakes me early. He wants to walk down by the river because he has some things he wants to tell me. He is whispering. I feel my stomach start balling up. The last time Papa said he wanted to talk with me, the news was about Mama and it was very bad.

I pull Peter's skinny little wrist off my arm. It's like sleeping with a rolling pin. He's always turning over and turning around, and besides that, I never have any covers, and I always have to check and see if he wet the bed. I roll away from him and up against Birdie. She opens her eyes and lets out a holler, the way she always does when she wakes up fast, as if the wake-up world is too hard to be in. I tell her, "Shush, Birdie. It's okay," even though I know it's not, because why else would Papa want to walk down by the river? Then Birdie falls back asleep, and I am the only one awake. Even our cat, Big Pumpkin Face, is sleeping, all curled up by my shoulder. I pretend I am asleep. I think about what my papa wants to tell me. My belly is a hard tight spring. Then Papa comes back and asks what I'm still in bed for.

I believe my bed wants me to stay. I listen to it, and

it tells me it does like my company very much. It starts humming that happy tune that makes me start to feel better about things. Then Papa is back and this time he says, "Charlie Anne," and it is not soft, it is mad with a lot of hurry around the edges. I get up and tell him I can't get dressed with him watching over me.

"I'll fire up the cookstove," he says, and he is gone, shutting the door so quiet you can hardly tell it was ever open at all.

I climb out of bed. I pull my nightgown off and take the dress I wear for chores off the hook. It is Ivy's old dress, and there are new rips from when Birdie and I went out to check on the blackberries. Mirabel wants me to get another year out of it, so she cut off the sleeves and made it over so it would tie up on my shoulders, but now it hangs funny and looks like what it used to be: a feed sack for chickens.

That's when Mirabel talked the first time to Papa about Eleanor, my aunt from Boston, and how she and Uncle Will still had some money—even though most everyone else around here has lost all of theirs. Maybe they could give us some, she said. But that made my papa so mad he kicked the compost bucket off our porch, and Mirabel got that big frown on her face and told me I had to clean it all up, the beet tops and the old oatmeal and the carrot peels, plus I had to mop the whole porch and the stairs, just because.

I have one other dress. It is the one I wore to my

mama's funeral at the little church over the hill last year. Now it is all balled up and hidden way at the bottom of the chest at the foot of our bed, underneath all the books Mama told me I would read someday.

My boots are on the porch, where Mirabel makes me leave them. No dirt in this house. Not anymore. The door to the barn is open a little, so I know Thomas has already milked Anna May and let her outside. He gets boy chores. He plows and plants and mucks out the barn and fixes the fences and pounds nails that need nailing everywhere. The only outside jobs Mirabel gives me are hanging up the laundry and beating the rugs and looking for eggs.

"I would be doing your mother a disservice if I didn't help you become a young lady," she tells me.

Mirabel wants to know why I don't know how to do more things. Like how come I don't know the fork goes on the left? How come I don't know about good manners and how girls are supposed to be quiet and generous and not boastful at all? I don't tell her Mama never told me about those things. She told me to practice my reading, because one day all the jumbled words would sort themselves out and I would be the best reader she knew. "Don't worry," she told me, tucking an armful of someday books into the chest. "Everything takes time, Charlie Anne."

Mirabel teaches me different things. She brought a

little book with her, *The Charm of Fine Manners*, and she keeps it in the pocket of her apron and she pulls it out at night after the supper dishes are done. "It is impossible for the selfish or ill-tempered girl to win love and friends," she reads. A moth thrashes against the inside of our screen door, and I get up to let it out.

Then Mirabel shows me how to make a vinegar pie that tastes almost like lemon pie because you need to know how to make things better when the hard times come, and Lord knows, they come. They come for everyone. That's what she tells me. I want her to stop talking about bad things.

"Are you listening?" Mirabel asks when she finds me on the porch, putting my boots on so I can go with Papa. "I want you to make one of those vinegar pies, the one your papa likes so much."

I am looking out at the river. It is all angry this morning. It is crashing over the big boulders. I wonder if it knows what my papa is going to tell me.

The grass is wet from the rain last night. I am walking behind Papa. His footsteps are very big. I can fit two of my steps in one of his.

For once, I don't want to go to the river. My papa says the river is a good place to talk about bad things. The river pulls all the bad words into the deep part and lets them sink to the bottom and then it carries them away. For this reason, I want to go back to bed. I do not want to hear any more bad things.

The river was Mama's favorite place. That is why her grave is on the hill, under her favorite oak tree. You can see way down the river and the tree keeps you all shaded and sometimes an acorn falls on your head. Those are lucky days, the acorn-falling-on-your-head days. They make you wise, Mama told me once.

Now I come here when Mama calls me. I tell her all about Mirabel and about how Ivy isn't turning out so well, now that she is a teenager. Mama tells me to try and put up with Mirabel so things go better for me. She tells me to let Ivy look at her *Movie Mirror* magazine if it makes her happy. She tells me Ivy is very lonely. I tell her it is no wonder, since no one wants to be with her.

A tiny grave stands beside us, for the baby who took Mama away. I try not to look at it much, seeing how that baby took Mama straight to heaven without time for any goodbyes at all.

Papa picks some daisies on the way. I know what he is doing. Whatever he is going to tell me, he is going to tell Mama, too.

We stop in front of Mama. I ask her what Papa is going to tell me. She does not answer me. I think she is wondering, too.

My legs are feeling like they are going to buckle right out from under me. I reach for Mama.

Papa sits down beside Mama. "Have a seat, Charlie Anne." He pats the ground next to Mama. I sit down. I know she is holding my hand, but I wish I could feel it better.

"I want you to keep an eye on those chickens, make sure they get enough corn so they keep laying eggs, Charlie Anne."

I wonder what he is getting at. I look out at the river. It is racing and flying over the boulders, knocking them so hard they move, and when they do, they are thunder booming. The river is very angry this morning.

"I noticed Bea was trying to hide her eggs under the blackberries."

He watches the river, but I am wondering why he is talking about chickens.

I look at Mama's grave, at the daisies, and then I notice Papa has put some daisies on Baby's grave. I reach over and push them back to Mama. I think about how maybe they should not have put Baby's grave so close.

"And make sure the coop is locked at night. You don't want that fox getting in there again. And keep Big Pumpkin Face away."

I sit back on my heels. I listen to the river pound. I hear my heart pound. I take a deep breath. Very slowly I ask, "Where are you going?"

"Well, that's the thing I am trying to get to, Charlie Anne. It will only be for a little while. I know you'll be fine." He doesn't say anything else, and we both watch the river thunder past.

"Where are you going?" I say again.

"I took a job building roads up north, Charlie Anne. There's work up there, now that President Roosevelt is doing something. I'm taking Thomas with me. It won't be for long."

The river crashes. My thoughts are all mixed up. I feel my heart get all worried and then mad and then start crashing inside of me like the river.

"You can't do that. You can't leave. Mama won't like that. She won't like that at all."

"Charlie Anne," says Papa. He rubs his hand through his hair the way he does when he does not know what to say next. Then he reaches up for me.

I pull away, and turn so he cannot see the tears that

are hurrying down my face. I wipe them away with the back of my arm.

He watches the river. It is crashing and roaring and furious. He keeps running his hand through his hair.

"Mama will be really mad. She told us our family was more important than anything, remember?"

The tears are falling down my face so fast I can't see anything. The boulders are thundering.

Papa is watching the river, too. Then he shakes his head. "I am keeping this family together, Charlie Anne. Try and understand. We're going to lose the farm if I don't do something. There are whole families sleeping under bridges in the city, that's how bad things are."

I can hardly believe it. I look at Mama's stone, at the name *Sylvie*. "Mama will be mad. Mama would want us to stay together, through thick and thin. Remember how she used to say blood is thicker than anything and you don't run out on one another?"

Papa makes that thin line with his lips. He started doing it after the funeral. "There are all different ways of keeping a family together, Charlie Anne."

I jump up and face him. "THROUGH IT ALL, A FAMILY STICKS TOGETHER!" I am roaring. I can't hear the river anymore.

"I know it, Charlie Anne."

Papa is still sitting, and he looks out at the river, and I think he has run out of things to say. Bluebirds fly over our heads. The color of their wings is so blue it can make you stop breathing. They were Mama's favorite birds.

"Look at that," says Papa, standing up. "I think your mama is telling us that it will be okay."

I stamp my foot. "No, she is not. She is saying she wants you to stay here. This is home. This is where the bluebirds are."

I do not even have to ask what his plan is, about who will take care of us. "You can't leave us with Mirabel. You know we hate her."

Papa sighs. "I need you to be brave, Charlie Anne. I need you to help Mirabel."

"I do not want to help Mirabel. I do not want to do so many chores all the time and I do not want her to teach me to be a young lady and I do not want you to go."

I think for a minute. "And how about Thomas? Mama would be really mad if she knew you were taking Thomas."

"Aren't you really mad, Mama?" I say, turning to her stone.

"Charlie Anne . . . ," says my papa. "Charlie Anne." He reaches for me, and for just a moment, I let him pull me so close I can smell the soap he uses to lather his face. But then I yank myself away, madder than the thundering river.

"Charlie Anne," he says again, but I turn away and cross my arms and will not look at him anymore.

I know he is waiting for me to rush toward him and let him hug me. But I stand right where I am. I won't look at him, either. After a long while, he sighs and starts walking away from me, toward the house. I turn and watch him go, and then I flop on the ground by Mama and cry so hard I cannot hear if she is saying anything to me or not.

Papa is yelling at Mirabel in the kitchen when I get back.

"I already told you, not Eleanor." He stomps out on the porch and slams the door. I feel my stomach start balling up.

Mirabel follows him outside. "And I keep telling you, it's the only way."

Papa kicks the compost bucket again. A whole bunch of coffee grounds and eggshells and potato peels go flying, and I think my papa better stop doing this. It clangs and flies off the porch and onto the front yard and rolls up next to me. I do not dare take another step.

Papa watches the bucket stop right beside my feet. Minnie and Olympia and Bea rush right over, and Olympia pecks Minnie and Bea out of the way to get to the oatmeal first.

Papa's lips are in that straight line. He turns back to Mirabel. "Not Eleanor. I will send money soon."

"A few dollars a month," says Mirabel. "What's that going to get us?"

Papa gives her one of his terrific bad looks, the kind he gives only to Anna May when she kicks the milk pail over, and then he storms back in the house. I hear him holler to Thomas to get moving. I am left wondering what they mean about my aunt Eleanor. I don't like her at all.

"Where have you been?" says Mirabel as soon as she sees me standing beside the compost pail. She is carrying a basket of wet clothes. "You and your father, taking off like that, on a morning like this, when we have so much to do to get ready for tomorrow. Why, I just don't understand you at all."

I think the barn is calling me, right now while I am looking at Mirabel and her big frown.

"What are you doing just standing there like that?"

I look down at all the compost all over the ground. There is leftover vegetable soup on my foot. I wipe it on the grass.

I built myself a secret place in the barn, high in the loft, and I want to go there now. I made it out of a stack of hay bales, and there is a secret opening against the wall so nobody can find me, and it is peaceful inside. I am glad just to be there. I made little window places for the sun to jump inside. I spread Mama's poppy-colored quilt on the floor, and when I lie down, I feel her hugging me. Also, I keep her hairbrush under the quilt. Sometimes I pull it out and brush my hair, and after about one thousand brushes, I begin to feel better about things.

"Charlie Anne, are you listening?" says Mirabel.

I jump a little and nod my head.

"Well, pick up that pail and clean up that mess and then come and help me hang up your father's clothes. We have to get everything hung up right quick if we want them to dry in time. I want to get a big picnic packed. Your father and Thomas are going to be on the road for a long while."

As I start cleaning up the potato peels, Mirabel lifts up the laundry basket and heads off to the clothesline, and I hear her shoes snap when she walks, even in the wet grass. They are so loud that I almost don't hear the clothesline start whimpering when she walks near.

Mirabel tells me I have to make Papa his favorite lunch. She tells me she doesn't care if I am mad at him or not. She has all this mending to do for Papa and Thomas, so I need to make lunch. I load up the cookstove with wood and let the coals get hot. Then I make eggs scrambled with browned onions, biscuits as high as I can make them, fried potatoes and pickled beets.

I make a vinegar pie for dessert, because it is Papa's favorite, and Mirabel tells me, "Don't forget the vinegar pie." I mix half a cup of butter with a cup and a quarter of sugar until it is light and fluffy, and then I add three eggs, two big tablespoons of cider vinegar and a teaspoon of vanilla. I pour it all into a pie crust and bake it in a warm oven for forty-five minutes until when I stick a knife in, the knife comes out clean.

Ivy crinkles her face when I put the pie on the table. I tell her I hope her nose gets stuck that way. I say this before Papa sits down. He would make me eat by myself. Treat others the way you want to be treated, he says all the time, over and over. I am pretty sure this is very easy if you do not have a sister like Ivy.

Papa comes to the table and then Thomas comes in from the barn and we all sit down and Papa bows his head and then we all have to fold our hands on our laps and then he says, "Bless this family." Then we have silent time that Papa says we should use to think about the good things in our lives, the things to be grateful about. Ivy usually rolls her eyes at this part and Birdie says, "Are we done yet?"

I don't tell Papa, but right now I am thinking about how my life isn't so good, how it isn't turning out the way I wanted, not at all. How Mama is still gone, even though every night I tell her couldn't she please be hugging me awake in the morning, but there's always only Peter rolling on top of me and Big Pumpkin Face curled up against my shoulder and Birdie crying out from her dreams and Ivy with her head under the pillow. That's all there ever is.

Papa tells Thomas he must take Peter out to the barn and make sure he knows every last thing there is to know about taking care of Anna May and Minnie and Olympia and Bea. "But I already know how to do everything," I say, taking a bite of pie so big my cheeks push out like an old hornpout fish. It is very good and does not taste like a hard-times pie at all. Ivy looks at me and rolls her eyes.

"Charlie Anne," says Papa, giving me that stern look because Mirabel is looking straight at him. "You're going to have to keep doing all the inside chores with Ivy and Mirabel."

"Ah, come on, Pa," says Thomas. "Charlie Anne can show Peter." Thomas is already on his second piece of pie. Food must run right through his belly, because he eats more than anyone and looks like a hickory stick. "I have to go get those traps."

Thomas and our neighbors, the Thatcher boys, trap on a spot upriver where I am not allowed to go. They trap otter and beaver, and I hate them for all the suffering.

"Show Peter," Papa tells Thomas, "and you can get the traps tomorrow before we go."

"And, Peter, I want you to keep a chart while I'm gone. Measure the corn and watch how high it is getting, week by week. I'll be interested to see that when I get home. And also how much milk Anna May is giving. I want you to keep track, okay?"

I look over at Papa. "But I do not want to do all the cooking and washing and ironing and everything. I hate inside chores. I know Anna May better than anyone. She'd give us more milk if I milked her."

Ivy giggles. Mirabel clears her throat. Her frown is very big. Papa keeps running his hand through his hair. He is looking all worn out. "Only until I get back," he says softly.

I give him my most terrible mad look. We'll just see about that.

After breakfast the next morning, Ivy gets up from the table and says she has to go to the privy awful bad. She said this after lunch yesterday and the day before.

"You get back here," I tell her.

"Shush," Papa says.

"But she never helps or anything," I tell him. "How many times does one person have to pee?"

"Charlie Anne," he says, "today is not the day for fighting."

I turn and face him. "You cannot leave me with her. I hate her, I really do."

"Charlie Anne," says Papa, his voice getting all

sharp. "Ivy is missing Mama, too. It is hard on every-one. You are not the only one." He gives me his most exasperated-with-Charlie Anne look, and I give him the one I save for only Ivy. Then he walks away and goes out to the barn to check on Thomas and Peter, and I shove my hands into the dishpan and hurry before the soap starts to sting.

When I am done, Mirabel says it is time to pack the lunch for Papa and Thomas. I go get the big basket Mama used to bring on picnics, where she would bring *Huckleberry Finn* and read to us while we ate cucumber sandwiches. Even Ivy was happy then. I would try and follow Mama's finger along while she read, but the letters would muddle together, and she would say it was all right, everything takes time.

I fill up the basket with biscuits and pie and baked potatoes and things that will keep overnight. When I go out to the barn to get the last of the apples from the apple barrel, Thomas is coming down the hill with the traps.

"You better not put them where Birdie can get them," I say.

He rolls his eyes. "What do you think, Charlie Anne, I don't have any sense at all?"

Then he dumps the traps in his wooden box, and they clang so loud Anna May jumps. Thomas hooks the latch shut and I watch to make sure he snaps it tight.

* * *

I give Anna May a real good look. She is lonely. I named her newest calf Belle, and now that calf is almost grown and living with Old Mr. Jolly across the road. I keep an eye on his fields to make sure he is treating her right, see if she's getting too skinny. Sometimes I go over and ask Old Mr. Jolly if he is treating her right. He tells me, "She is a cow, Charlie Anne." I tell him, "She is a good cow and her name is Belle and you better take good care of her, or else." He tells me I better mind my manners and stop telling him what to do or he will tell my papa that I am not respecting my elders.

We'll just see about that. I tell on Old Mr. Jolly.

Papa says Old Mr. Jolly has been lonely since his wife died all those years ago. But maybe he'll cheer up because he is getting a new wife, a cousin of the wife he buried. She is from Mississippi. I tell Papa I do not care about a new wife. Old Mr. Jolly better be good to Belle or I am taking her back.

"You can't do that, Charlie Anne. You can't get something back that's already gone."

"We'll just see about that," I tell him.

Anna May has been a real crab ever since Belle was sold to Old Mr. Jolly. I told Papa it was a very bad idea. He told me we needed the money. Mama was still with us then and I asked her what for, why did we need the money. Mama said we needed to buy new wire for fencing. I told her we did not need new wire. Anna May would stay put if I told her.

"Oh, Charlie Anne," Mama said. "Things are getting hard out in the world right now. We're lucky, living on this farm, but it's starting to get bad for us. We need some things. You could really use new boots, too."

I looked down at my boots. They were the ones Thomas used to wear, and I pushed cardboard down inside to cover the holes and stuffed them with rags to make them fit. "I would rather keep Belle."

Then my mama hugged me like she always did and she gave me a piece of pudding cake and some buttermilk and then I started feeling better. "Belle is only going next door to Mr. Jolly's and you can watch her. I bet she'll be happy over there with all those fields. Did you see all the buttercups growing?"

Mama said that to get my mind off things. She knew I love buttercups.

The thing about Old Mr. Jolly is he is not old. He is just one of those men who gets gray hair really early and he mostly keeps to himself, and since he does not have a wife to tell him to stand up straight, he started walking bent over like a willow twig way before he should have. That's what Papa said. Wives are a good thing, he said, winking at my mama.

Thinking about my mama makes even my toes feel sad, so I get the milk stool and the pail and set them down, being careful of Anna May's kicking foot. "Peter is not going to steal my job away from me," I tell Anna May.

"Papa told me to show Peter all this, not you," says Thomas, walking up behind me. I know he is saying this because I am a girl.

"I know how to milk a cow," I tell him. "And I know you're supposed to do this first thing in the morning. How come you waited?"

Anna May is giving me grumpy looks. "Oh, don't you be looking at me that way," I tell her, giving her some grain to keep her mind off things. "Blame Thomas." I am very stern with her or else she will get too bossy and then she will think she can kick me the way she sometimes kicks Papa when he is thinking about Mama.

I have to set the pail right or Anna May will kick it right out of the barn. I sit down on the stool and I tell her she better be good, or else. She just stands there chewing the way she always does, her eyes that same soft molasses color as Belle's, and I look up at Thomas and show him, this is how you milk a cow.

When I am nearly done and feeling all good about things, that's when I start softening up, and Anna May must feel me not being stern with her anymore and that's when she lets her kicking foot fly and she sends the milk bucket crashing against the wall. Milk spills all over me and Thomas hollers and I know Mirabel is going to be very mad. I give Anna May my most terrible mad look. She doesn't act sorry at all.

Birdie does not understand things like sometimes when people go away, they really do come back, so I scoop her up and put her on my hip. "Where's Papa going?" she keeps asking.

"He's going up north to build roads, Birdie."

She likes to stay in that faraway place pretty much all the time now, ever since Mama left us, so she does not really hear what I say.

"Where's Thomas going?" she asks.

"He's going to work with Papa."

"It won't be for long," Papa says, coming up and giving Birdie and me a big hug at the same time. I stiffen up like Mirabel's sheets.

"I'll bring more of these when I come," Papa tells Birdie, dropping a lemon drop in her hands, and she can hardly quit her giggling long enough to get it in her mouth.

Then Papa turns to Peter. Peter stands up straight and sticks his chest out like a rooster. He shakes Papa's hand. "Don't forget, I want to know how that corn is growing, week by week," Papa tells him.

At the last minute, Papa remembers he wanted us to

all trace our feet on paper so he could send back some new shoes as soon as he gets paid. He lays out paper on the ground and gives us a pencil, and since we are not wearing shoes, it only takes a minute.

Ivy has her magazine in her pocket, and it falls out when she is tracing her feet. Mirabel brought it to get a head start on nice feelings with Ivy. I knew what she was up to.

Before I know it, Papa is right up beside me. "I'm sorry, Charlie Anne, I really am," he is saying, and I am already blocking my ears.

"Mama's really going to be mad," I say, and I feel a little bit mean telling him this, and even more mean when I turn away and won't let him hug me. He stands for a minute waiting for me to turn around and hug him, but I do not budge because I am the boulder in the middle of the river now, which nothing can move, not even Papa.

Then he sighs and tells Thomas to hurry up with hugging Peter, and then it's time for them to get going and they start walking down the driveway, and every one of us is standing there waving, everyone but me. Papa turns around one last time and I know he is looking especially at me, but I am the boulder again. Then Peter sobs and flies after them and jumps up into Papa's arms, and Papa lets him stay there for a minute before sending him back to Mirabel.

Then they are off to Evangeline's General Store, where they are going to get a ride with some other men from town who are heading north to build roads.

"Mama is really mad," I whisper as I watch Papa and Thomas walk away.

Mirabel says enough waving, she needs some help. Thank God the garden's in, and the peas are ready. She sends Ivy and Peter and Birdie to get the peas and hoe for a while. Me, I get more laundry. Yesterday Mirabel wanted me to read from her little manners book, but I kept mixing up the words and she pulled the book away and read it to me:

> To prepare herself rightly to fulfill
> all the duties that belong to the
> mistress of a home should be the
> one all-embracing aim of any
> young girl's life . . .

We'll just see about that, I think as Mirabel gets a fire started out by the clothesline and I pull water up from the bucket in the well and dump it into the big kettle. While we wait for it to heat up, I carry more water for the rinsing.

Here is how the job is done: You heat up the water until it is steaming and very hot, and then you dump the clothes in with plenty of soap and let them soak a good long while. Be careful not to get burned, you have to tell yourself over and over, and then you have to stir everything with the same paddle your great-grandmother used, because that is the way these chores are done, the same way, over and over, for a thousand years. Then when the clothes are cool enough to touch, you rub them against the washboard until your hands are red and raw, and then you put everything in the rinse bucket and stir some more until you get every last bit of soap out.

Mirabel leaves me as soon as the water cools enough so I will not get burned, and she covers the fire with dirt, and then I have to get all the clothes hung up and the water from the buckets dumped out.

The clothesline is all fed up that I am making it so heavy with all these clothes on such a hot day, and Minnie and Olympia and Bea are pecking in the dirt around my feet, and I am thinking this is one of the worst days of my life, and that's when I hear Mama calling me, telling me that maybe I might want to come up and visit for a while.

I don't tell Mirabel where I am going. I just start running. When I pass by Ivy, she is sitting in the dirt, looking at all the peas she still has to pick.

"Wait," she yells.

I do not wait.

* * *

When I get to the river, I am out of breath. I go up and
sit by Mama and rest for a minute, and then I tell her
about my awful day, and she tells me she already knows
about it all, but I can tell her some more if it will make
me feel better. So I tell her about how I did not hug
Papa or anything and now he is going to be gone for a
very long time. She says it is all right. She knows Papa
understands.

I tell her I think Mirabel has her eyes on Papa in a
bad way, and that makes Mama giggle. *You don't need to
worry about that*, Mama tells me. Then she tells me not
to be too sad about all the other things that happened
today because good things are right around the corner.
I ask her what they are and she tells me she cannot say.
They are secrets.

I like secrets, I tell her.

Me too, she says.

We sit for a long time just watching the river. It is
swirling and churning and I think it is still terribly
angry and in an awful hurry to rush away from here.

When I get home, Mirabel is sitting at the table,
writing. I walk up close and try and read the letters, but
they are mostly all jumbled up, except I know what the
word *Eleanor* looks like.

"It's for the best" is all she says, and she dips her pen
in the ink and starts writing again.

"Papa said not Aunt Eleanor." I give Mirabel my most terrible mad look.

"Have you no manners at all?" asks Mirabel, reaching in her pocket for the book that is hidden there.

7

I hear Belle bellowing in Old Mr. Jolly's field when I am weeding in the cucumber patch. I think she is calling to her mama, Anna May, and I can tell Anna May thinks so, too, because she looks up from the clover she is munching and goes and haves herself a look.

Then I go have myself a look. I am wondering where Old Mr. Jolly is and why he isn't doing something about Belle.

No wonder Belle is yelling her head off! She is standing in the brier patch all tangled up. I feel ashamed of Old Mr. Jolly, that he is not taking very good care of Belle. He let his fence get so bad without fixing it, and now Belle has wandered down to the brier patch alone and gotten herself all stuck. She is bellowing. I told Papa that Belle would come to no good living with Old Mr. Jolly.

Anna May starts mooing and I know she is telling Belle, what the dickens are you doing in that brier patch? I know this because I have listened to Anna May for so long that I can tell what she is saying, even when I don't put my ear to her heart. She's that kind of cow. She tells things like they are. If she is hungry, she tells you, what are you taking so long for? If she does not want to be milked, she kicks the bucket. If she is clear worn out from all the milk she has been making, she'll go have herself a good nap under the butternut tree, and she won't get up for nobody. When you find her and yell, "What are you doing there under that butternut tree?" she will tell you she is taking a nap, whatever does it look like? Anna May is that kind of cow.

Now Anna May is bellowing and Belle is bawling. I wonder where Old Mr. Jolly is, why he isn't doing something about Belle being stuck in the brier patch.

"Oh, Belle," I say, hurrying across the road and over the fence that runs on Old Mr. Jolly's side of the road.

I can tell even before I get to Belle that it is worse than I was thinking. Briers tangle around her legs, and there is blood, and deerflies are buzzing all over the hurting places. As soon as I get up to her, she stomps around and she gets herself even more tangled, and then a dozen flies start pestering me.

A cow caught in a brier patch is one of the saddest things you ever will see. Belle's soft honey-brown legs are wrapped up in thorns, and somehow she has gotten one of the big branches stuck on her back and another on her chest. My heart is sobbing, just looking at her.

Anna May waits for me to tell her how Belle got stuck in that brier patch. I'm still not sure yet, but I know it is all Old Mr. Jolly's fault.

Papa says a cow needs a big bell. Anna May has one.

We hear her when she walks around, and it is easy to find her on those days she decides she wants to eat clover for a little longer and not come down to the barn. Old Mr. Jolly never bothered with a bell, so I have nothing to hold on to. I yell up at the house to see where he is, but even the windows are shut up tight. "Where is he?" I ask Belle. She is too upset to have a conversation about Old Mr. Jolly.

I grab around her neck and try to pull her because now while I've been standing here, she has got her head all tangled up in the briers, too. "You have no sense," I tell her. She starts bawling her head off after that, and I tell her I am sorry for saying that, but when you think about it, you know I am right.

I go behind her then and give her a big push and get briers caught around my hand, and I start bleeding something awful. Then I start jumping around and sucking on my fingers while Belle stands snorting mad that I'm not helping her quicker. I push her again and she takes a baby step forward, then stops and starts bawling like a baby. Then Anna May calls over, what is taking so long?

"You better get yourself out of there before I count ten," I tell Belle. I give her my most terrible mad look. She watches me for a moment, then Anna May yells that she better start moving, and I give her another push. I push again and start thinking about how maybe

I should go hunt for a branch to give Belle a you-know-what on the backside, but then Belle looks over at me like she knows what I am thinking, and I feel ashamed of myself for even thinking about a you-know-what, and so I walk around and gaze right into her soft molasses eyes.

"Look, Belle. Some things you just have to do yourself. That's what Mama tells me. Now, I can help you a little bit, get some of these briers off you if you'll stand still, but you have to do the rest yourself. I can give you a little push, but you have to get yourself out of this brier patch. Do you understand me?"

Belle shakes her head and I know she is telling me her legs are hurting and I need to hurry up. So I reach up and pat her neck and start pulling the big brier off her back and while I am doing this I tell her how pretty she is this morning and when I am done telling her that I move over and start pulling the brier off her chest and that's when I tell her it's almost time for her to think about that nice cool spot over by the stone wall where she likes to lie down right in the middle of the buttercups and have herself a nap. Then I am so careful pulling the briers off her front legs and then her back legs, but I still get myself stuck pretty bad.

Anna May bawls again and Belle decides enough is enough. She runs like a nervous Nellie out of that brier patch, and before I can even get myself untangled, she is at the barn. I run after her, and when I get to her, I am ready to give her my stay-out-of-the-brier-patch lecture, but I think she already knows that on her own.

I let her stand there for a minute and go find out what's the matter with Old Mr. Jolly and how come he's taking such bad care of Belle.

He is not in the barn or around the chicken coop, and then I go knock pretty loud on his front door, and when no one comes, I go around to the back door and kick it for a while. I look in the windows and see all his dishes are washed and put on the rack to dry, and the cookstove is polished and there is a new cloth on the table, and come to think of it, even his windows are washed.

"Humph," I tell Belle when I catch up to her by the stone wall. "What do you think about that?" She doesn't say much, so I tell her why doesn't she come home with me since it looks like Old Mr. Jolly doesn't know two bits about taking care of cows.

Anna May bellows as soon as she hears us coming across the road. Belle hurries over to her and nestles up to her, happy as a fiddle. Anna May is making moon eyes at Belle, and licking her. I press my face against Belle, smelling her soft neck. She is very happy. "Sometimes you just need your mama," I tell her.

8

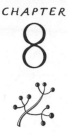

Olympia, Minnie and Bea forget all about how they are chickens and how they are supposed to be laying eggs, and now we have nothing to trade for the few groceries that Mirabel wants to buy at Evangeline's store.

So Mirabel comes up with another idea. "It will be like we're trading eggs, only you can go to Evangeline's and say you'll sweep the floors if she will give us some flour and sugar, and maybe some coffee, on credit." Mirabel is telling me this while she is frying up the last of the salt pork.

We have not heard from Papa, and the salt pork and one old ham butt is all that's left in the smokehouse. Mirabel has a big frown mostly all the time.

"Is that all you got?" she says when she notices the bucket of strawberries I put on the table. I have been berrying in the hot morning sun, trying to keep away from yellow jackets.

"That's all there were." Birdie starts tugging on my dress as soon as Mirabel says Evangeline's because she likes the lemon drops so much.

"Are you sure that's all there were?" Mirabel is checking my face for lying.

"I'm not Ivy," I say. "That's all there were."

I sit down on the chair and look at my feet, no shoes all summer. I don't want to go to Evangeline's and ask for credit. "Papa doesn't do that," I tell Mirabel.

"Don't Papa me," she says. "We haven't heard from him in weeks, and we need credit until we hear from Eleanor."

I tell Mirabel we do not need Aunt Eleanor. Mirabel tells me I am too big for my britches. I tell her I am not wearing britches, I am wearing a dress. Then I scoot Birdie out the door and tell Peter and Ivy we have to all go to Evangeline's.

As we are hurrying down the driveway, Olympia, Minnie and Bea are sunning themselves on the manure pile. I tell them they better stop lazing around and lay some eggs or they will get the what-for as soon as I get home.

Evangeline is looking like she is not used to people asking her for credit. But I know folks are asking her all the time now that half the men in our town are working on roads for President Roosevelt. It is hard now for everybody.

She is rubbing her forehead. We are standing beside big bags of flour that nobody bought yet. That can't be good: to have flour that nobody wants. I look at the lemon drops in the candy case. When you have flour you can't sell, you can't be giving away lemon drops, either.

"I don't know about credit," Evangeline says, coming around closer to us. "Where's Mirabel?"

"Home," I tell her. "Home because she hasn't had a minute off her feet all day. That's what she told us to say." Ivy walks off to check where the movie magazines are and Birdie is in her far-off place, looking at the lemon drops.

"I would like to help you children, really I would, but it's getting really hard for me now, too."

"But we're really good sweepers," I tell her. "And our papa promised to send money soon. Mirabel says we'll pay you as soon as we hear from Papa."

While Evangeline goes through her head thinking what she should do, Becky Ellis and her mother walk in, and Birdie takes one look at them and runs over to hide behind me. The Ellis family can do that to a person.

Becky sticks her nose straight in the air when she sees me and I hope it gets stuck way up there. Then she gives her nose a pinch, like something in the store smells really bad, probably me.

I look Becky in the face and let all those times Papa told us about kindness and compassion and treating others the way you want to be treated rush right out the window, and I stick my tongue out at her. It feels almost as fine as having a cool sweet lemon drop in my mouth.

That's when Evangeline brings up the subject of our credit again, and now I wish she would forget the whole thing.

"What do you need again?" asks Evangeline.

"Lemon drops," whispers Birdie, tugging on my arm.

"Flour," I say, my voice all balled up inside of me. "And sugar and maybe some coffee . . . and a lemon drop for Birdie."

Then Evangeline sighs and turns and whispers to Mrs. Ellis that she can't very well let Sylvie's children go hungry—poor things—and then she tells me to go get the brooms in the back closet and get to work.

Mrs. Ellis is looking at our bare feet. Maybe I should not have run through so many mud puddles on the way here. I want to pull Becky's tie-up shoes and her stockings right off her feet. Then I notice Birdie's feet. She jumped in every single puddle, and her feet, as tiny and perfect as a sparrow's, are dirtier than mine. I take her hand and pull her away from those Ellis eyes and go get the brooms.

Becky's mama keeps writing letters to very important people telling them we still don't have a teacher way up here. Times are hard, the very important people keep telling her. "My daughter can't grow up without a proper education," she tells us all, and after she says this about a dozen Sundays in a row while standing up in her fancy box pew in front of everybody at church, you can tell people are surely kind of embarrassed and shameful over our situation, but knowing at the same time that most of the men are gone now and how the rest of us need to work together because of how bad things are getting, we tell ourselves that there will be time for school when times are better.

Our schoolhouse has been all boarded up for more than a year now, ever since Miss Moran told us she was going as far away from our town as she could get. Maybe California, is the last thing she said before she hurried away. I was so happy she left I did cartwheels all the way to the upper field, and Anna May wanted to know why I wasn't walking on my feet, the way the Lord intended.

My papa said things are no better in California. It's bad everywhere. We're luckier than most, way up here, because we all have a cow in the field and chickens in the coop, and apples on the trees and peas and corn and potatoes in the garden. He stood up in church one Sunday before he left and faced us all. "There's a colored lady teaching school four towns over, that's what I've heard. If we're lucky, maybe she can help us find someone who would come out here soon as the hay is in and teach the children through the winter."

Mrs. Ellis jumped up so fast you would have thought she was sitting on something. "You are all backwater people without a wit of sense. That's why no one decent wants to come teach us. And we certainly aren't going to improve our situation by having a colored teacher in our town. I'm ready to send my girl to Boston, where they know how to educate children properly." She looked at Becky, with her hair all curled and her shoes all shining, and Becky grinned.

Papa said under his breath that might not be a bad idea.

I miss my papa very much.

I give Peter a broom and tell him to sweep the porch on Evangeline's store, and I give Ivy a broom and tell her to sweep in the front. She takes one look at it and tells me she isn't sweeping up this dirty old floor, and she stomps off and goes over by the table where sometimes Evangeline keeps *Movie Mirror* magazines. But there are none. I see her looking at her dress and at the holes that run through it and then over at Becky, who is wearing a dress so new it still has a pin sparkling near the hem that her mama must have forgot. I hope Becky gets pricked pretty bad. Serves her right when the rest of us are wearing the same handing-me-down-forevers we always get.

I take Birdie's hand and we go sweep over by the woodstove that heats the store in winter, and Birdie keeps asking me if I think we'll get some lemon drops. I tell her sometimes you get things you wish for. You really do. Life is like that sometimes.

I sweep all along the wooden floor and beneath the shelves that hold flour and laundry soap and bluing rinse. There are kerosene lanterns and dustpans hanging on big hooks, and china dishes stacked on the table beside cups and bowls, and fifty-pound bags of sugar beside a barrel of sauerkraut and a barrel of pickles.

Mrs. Ellis is looking over dress fabric when Zella Polanski walks in. She lives up the road and must have seen Mrs. Ellis out walking. Then Mrs. Reilly comes. They are just like Minnie and Olympia and Bea. When one comes, they all come running. Now all they need is a manure pile.

They stand by the fabric, whispering, and pretty soon Evangeline walks over to talk to them all.

"Have you heard?"

"What?" asks Mrs. Ellis.

"They were to be married this morning. He went to the train station to pick her up and then they were to be married, all without barely knowing each other. She's from Mississippi, you know."

"What would anyone want to come way up here for?" says Zella.

"Especially to marry *that* man," says Mrs. Ellis, and I do not even have to hear another word to know who it is they are talking about.

"Oh, come now, ladies," says Evangeline. "He's been without a wife for so many years; surely he deserves a little happiness."

"I don't know who would want him, though," says Mrs. Reilly. "I bet he hasn't cut his hair in six months."

"Or shaved," laughs Zella.

I stand there sweeping, wondering who would want Old Mr. Jolly when he can't even take care of a cow.

"We'll find out soon enough," says Evangeline. She starts packing up our flour and sugar and a little coffee. Birdie is mooning over the lemon drops so bad I think her face is going to fall off.

Mrs. Ellis pulls a grape pop from the icebox, opens it on the bottle opener that's nailed to the wall and hands the bottle to Becky. We all just about faint from looking at the fizzing purple as Becky holds the bottle up to the sun. Then she smiles over at us, puts it up to her mouth and takes a huge gulp.

"The electric is coming," Becky tells me after she drinks half her pop. "We are the only family on our road that's getting the electric and the telephone at the same time."

Then she takes another gulp, and if I still prayed to the angels, I would pray for something very bad to happen to her.

Evangeline notices, too, and then she pulls a small bag of lemon drops out of the basket and drops it in my hand, and I pass the candies out and I think about how life is like that sometimes. Sometimes you do get what you hope for.

This is how I make sure I am the first to see Old Mr. Jolly's new wife.

I run to my swing as many times a day as I can get away from Mirabel and her chores and her manners book. I start pumping my legs and look over at Belle and Anna May, who are resting under the butternut tree. I ask them if they are sick of hearing all about how a young lady must avoid a loud tone of voice, and also avoid laughing too much and too easily. They tell me they are.

I get to pumping and swinging high enough to look straight into our loft and watch Big Pumpkin Face soak up the sun on a pile of hay, and when I get up just a little higher, I can poke my head out and see clear up our road, almost all the way to Evangeline's store.

And then wouldn't you know it: late in the day when Mirabel is napping and Ivy is supposed to be picking string beans, I see Old Mr. Jolly's truck coming down the road.

I am so excited about seeing somebody new I can hardly breathe. Spending all day, every day, with only Ivy and Peter and Birdie and especially, *especially*

Mirabel is like eating the same plate of peas, every day, all day, morning, noon and night.

I try and keep my legs pumping high so I can get a good look at Old Mr. Jolly's wife. Higher, higher, higher I push my legs. Higher, higher, higher my swing goes. At the split second Old Mr. Jolly's truck is close enough for me to almost see in the front window (are there three people in there?) my swing starts going down. So quick as I can, I push my legs and then I am up, up, up again, looking past our barn, and I see Old Mr. Jolly pull into the driveway and get out and go around to open the door on the other side of the truck, and, hey, wait a minute, who's that sitting in the middle?

Then I am going down again, and I give my legs a good talking to and get myself back up again. A lady climbs out of the truck and she is wearing trousers, and they are red pepper red. I never saw a lady wearing trousers before, except maybe overalls sometimes for chores. I wonder if where she comes from in Mississippi all the ladies wear trousers.

Of course, just as these thoughts are filling up my head, my swing is going down again, so I kick my feet as hard as I believe possible because I want to see who else is in the truck, and that is a mistake because just as I am getting myself higher than I've ever been before, I hear something crack and I feel something snap and I go sailing in the direction of Old Mr. Jolly's new wife.

* * *

My knees grind into the gravel and little bits of stone cut the skin on my shoulder and my cheek as I roll over and over on the road, and finally when I come to a stop, I am lying with my arm underneath me.

Old Mr. Jolly's new wife is screaming, as if maybe she isn't too used to seeing girls go flying off their swings and landing in the middle of the road.

"Sweet Jesus," Old Mr. Jolly is saying.

I am all knocked out and I want to cry but I don't know how. I also cannot tell them that I am not dead.

Pretty soon after that, Old Mr. Jolly reaches under and picks me up and carries me into his house and sets me on the couch. I notice he has cut his hair and trimmed his beard. He is wearing a suit, which is surely something I've never seen him in before. The new Mrs. Jolly tucks a pillow under my head.

Then there is a lot of hurrying around on the new Mrs. Jolly's part and a lot of movement of my arm, and it does hurt something awful, and it seems I am still knocked out because I can't quite remember how to talk. So I don't.

"At least it's not broke," I hear Old Mr. Jolly say.

"You better go get her mother," the new Mrs. Jolly says, and then I hear Old Mr. Jolly tell her to shush because there isn't any mother, not anymore, and I am fading out while I am trying to tell him, yes, yes there is. She lives up on the hill by the river now.

"Her father is building roads."

"Then who does she live with?"

I hear Old Mr. Jolly groan, and I think in my half-asleep knocked-out way that I didn't know anyone else thought Mirabel was as bad as I did. I hear the new Mrs. Jolly talking again, and I think her voice is as soft as the buttercups sound when they wake each other in the morning.

Soon the new Mrs. Jolly is mopping my face and washing my arm and my knees with warm soapy water, and that's when I start opening my eyes, just a little teeny sliver at a time. Then Old Mr. Jolly is propping me up and the new Mrs. Jolly is trying to get me to drink some water, and that's when I see there is someone else in the room.

10

I open and shut my eyes a whole bunch of times because I never saw a colored girl up close before.

She is washing my arm, the one that was stuck under me when I fell on top of it, and it is hurting something awful now, and I jump quite a bit when I see who it is who is washing me. I wonder if she is the maid.

"Stop moving," she tells me, sounding a little bossy.

I try and move my arm, but it wants to stay put. I tell it that if maybe it moves a little, it will not hurt so bad, and if it wants to get back to swinging, it better start moving when I tell it. It pretends it cannot hear me.

While I am talking to my arm, the girl is watching me. She looks about my age, and she has little braids that stick out every which way all over her head, and I am wondering how she gets them to do that. She is wearing the same red pepper red trousers as the new Mrs. Jolly, and there is not a single patch or rip in them and not even a stain from picking strawberries or hunting for Minnie, Olympia, and Bea. I remember the chore dress I am wearing and I tell my arm to move a little so I can cover up the new rips from the brier patch. My arm doesn't listen and I have to watch the girl notice all the holes.

When she catches me looking at her, she looks right back at me without even a blink. I make a face when she gets to my elbow because it is hurting so bad, and she asks me what I am crying for.

"I am not crying," I say, moving a little, and I knock the dishpan of bloody water over on the floor. Old Mr. Jolly gets towels and mops everything up, and the new Mrs. Jolly asks him to go get more water from the well, and he comes back with another pailful so we can start all over.

"I am Rosalyn," says the new Mrs. Jolly. "This is Phoebe."

The girl doesn't look up. She keeps wiping my arm, and it hurts so bad I have to clamp my teeth together so I don't cry.

Becky Ellis had a maid once. Her father brought a colored man and his wife up from South Carolina to help on the farm, but they left before the first snow and Mrs. Ellis told us all at church that our town is too backwater for even a colored family.

While I am thinking on this, the new Mrs. Jolly starts in on my feet. I jump, but she is ready for me this time and is holding the dishpan tight. I want her to stop. My face is burning red that she is washing my feet, because I have not washed them in three days. I don't want the colored girl to look at them, either. I try and move them out of the way, but the new Mrs. Jolly is holding on.

I wish I had Becky Ellis's white-as-china feet right about now, I am thinking, and my eyes start filling up when I remember Mama telling me I should not be wanting what other people have. I better quit my belly-aching over what I don't have and be proud of who I am.

Now I squeeze my eyes real tight because I don't want the colored girl to see me crying, and I try and be proud of my feet. I am thinking about my feet so hard that when I hear singing, I think it is my mama trying to make me feel better.

It is not. It is the new Mrs. Jolly. She is singing so soft I am sure now it is the same sound I hear the buttercups use to wake each other up in the morning.

Then the girl opens her mouth and sings:

> *Farther along*
> *We'll know all about it,*
> *Farther along*
> *We'll understand why.*
> *Cheer up, my sister,*
> *Live in the sunshine,*
> *We'll understand it*
> *All by and by.*

I never did hear an angel sing before but now I do. The girl sings higher than the new Mrs. Jolly and brighter and it's like a bell ringing and she goes on and on, louder and louder, and before I know it my heart is flying up, up, up where Mama is and my soul splits in two and I do not know if I can get myself back together again. I would like to pinch myself to see if I have died and gone straight to be with Mama, but I cannot move my arm. Even Mr. Jolly is amazed. He has to sit down, it is so beautiful.

I can't stop looking at the girl. I watch her hard to see if she is real or not. Then she sings some more and she rubs my arm at the same time and she forgets what she is doing and rubs too hard and it hurts and I make up my mind that she is no angel. She only sings like one.

The new Mrs. Jolly dips the cloth in the water again and then uses it to get the little stones out of the cracks that the road left in my cheek. It hurts something awful and I can't help but yell out.

"What are you doing, flying in your swing so high like that?"

"I wanted to see what you looked like," I whisper. I don't tell her that I wanted to see her first, even before Ivy and Peter and Birdie.

"You were hoping to get a peek at me, were you?" She laughs and looks over at Old Mr. Jolly. "Was I what you expected?"

I look at her face. Her hair is the color of oak leaves in the fall, and it is not all pinned up like the other ladies wear or bobbed short like Becky Ellis cut her hair to look like in the movie magazines. It goes all over the

place in more curls than you could ever count, and I believe a hummingbird would summersault, it would be so happy to get inside there.

"Maybe if you were wearing trousers, your knees wouldn't look like shredded cheese," the new Mrs. Jolly whispers.

I never thought about a girl wearing trousers before, and then the girl says that maybe I should have a red pair to match all my cuts, and she giggles. Then she asks me if I know that Old Mr. Jolly is going to build her a rope swing that will be twenty feet high and it will start in the hayloft and swing out all the way to the road and do I want to come and try it with her and I tell her I am not sure if Mirabel will let me play with a colored girl or not.

Things get suddenly quiet. I think maybe that was the wrong thing to say and I wish my mama were here telling me what I should do now because the new Mrs. Jolly is reaching for the girl's shoulder and squeezing it and Old Mr. Jolly is clearing his throat a few times.

I am not sure if I should say I'm sorry, so I try and think about something different. I wonder about Old Mr. Jolly and about the new Mrs. Jolly and about why she likes him and about how can he possibly take care of a new wife when he can't even take care of a cow.

I wonder if she likes this house. I wonder if someone who wears red pepper red trousers would like a plain-as-potatoes house like this. You can tell Old Mr. Jolly scrubbed everything before he went to get her. But no matter how hard you wash, you can't hide chipped tables and chairs and how even the sofa is all worn out, and you can never get the tired old roses on the wallpaper to bloom again.

Then Old Mr. Jolly says that since I am sitting up now he is going out to check on the animals, see if the Thatcher boy did a good job or not, and before he gets out the door, I tell him the Thatcher boy did not. He did not do a good job with Belle. And how could he? He is a snake, and once a snake always a snake, and how can Old Mr. Jolly not know that? I tell him how Belle got all tangled up in the brier patch and how Old Mr. Jolly should be keeping better care of her than that. "I told Papa that Belle would come to no good over here."

"Well," says Old Mr. Jolly. His ears are getting all red in front of the new Mrs. Jolly.

"You better take better care of your new wife than you do of Belle," I say, looking at the new Mrs. Jolly.

For some reason, everyone thinks this is pretty funny. First the new Mrs. Jolly bursts out laughing, then Old Mr. Jolly starts in, and finally, Phoebe, which makes me kind of mad to have her laughing at me. Then Old Mr. Jolly says he better go outside and have a look at Belle. I don't tell him she is back with Anna May.

The new Mrs. Jolly brings over a plate of doughnuts. I haven't had any since my mama used to fry them for Sunday breakfast. These are filled with nutmeg and rolled in cinnamon sugar. We haven't had fancy spices like this in a long time. I eat three.

Then Old Mr. Jolly comes back in the house and says, "Charlie Anne, why is my cow in your field?"

I look up at him and tell him that sometimes cows need their mamas, even when they are looking all grown-up. I know he is about to tell me that children should have more sense than to take someone else's cow home with them, but the new Mrs. Jolly puts her arm on Old Mr. Jolly's shoulder and whispers that she and Phoebe don't like milk much anyway and maybe it would be all right for just a little while if the cow stayed with me, and suddenly I know without a shadow of a doubt that I am going to love the new Mrs. Jolly.

11

Right away, as soon as my belly is full of cinnamon-nutmeg doughnuts and I can move my arm and get my body up off Old Mr. Jolly's worn-out sofa, I have to go tell Mama all about Rosalyn and Phoebe.

You would be amazed, I tell her. I sit down carefully, trying not to let any little bits of grass get in my cuts. I ask her if she could hear them singing, and she tells me she could. She asks me how my cuts are and I tell her they are pretty bad.

Mama and I look out at the river together. It is fast-moving, and every so often we see a fish jump. I lie back and rest next to Mama and I tell her Rosalyn's voice is soft like the buttercups, and about her trousers. Did you ever see a lady wearing trousers? I ask. Mama tells me no, not like those, but trousers make a lot of sense when you think about it.

And then I get around to Phoebe. I'm not sure how to say it, but since it is Mama, I can just blurt it out. Phoebe is colored, I say.

I know, says Mama softly.

She sings like the angels taught her how to do it, I tell her.

I know, I heard her, too, says Mama.

Mama sighs, then I sigh. Mama says, *Phoebe lost her mama, too.*

How do you know that?

I just know. Maybe you can ask her about it when you see her again.

Maybe. She's a little bossy, though.

Mama laughs softly. *Sometimes people who've lost someone can be a little bossy.*

We are both quiet, watching the river. I miss Papa, I tell her, and she tells me she misses him, too. Then I snuggle closer to Mama. I am so happy just to be with her.

Then I hear Mama sigh that happy sigh you sigh when the sky is blue and the grass is getting long and the birds are singing and everything is starting to go a little right in the world again and I forget all about how my knees and my arm hurt and then I sigh right along with her.

Old Mr. Jolly is going to build her a swing, I tell Mama.

Is that so?

Mmmmmm, I say, but it better not go over the brier patch, and while he's at it, I wonder if he'll fix mine? Then I feel my eyes get a little heavy and my heart feel a little full and I start feeling all soft and snuggled up to Mama, with the sun shining down all over me, and

Mama says, *You're a wonder, Charlie Anne,* and I smile deep inside. Then I tell myself it would be good to take just a little nap. Mirabel won't even know.

Peter is sitting on the think-about-it chair by the wood box on the porch, and when I ask him "How come?" he gives me a mad look, and when I ask him "How come?" again, he says Mirabel made him because he stomped on her hatbox.

"How come?" I ask again, and this time he tells me he stomped on her hatbox because she made him hang out the towels and then go pick beet greens because she couldn't find me.

"I was supposed to be fixing the fence. I was measuring new posts," he says. "Where were you for so long, anyway?"

I make a mad-as-a-yellow-jacket face at him. Just because there are towels to hang or beet greens to pick, why does it have to be my job? Also, he doesn't see my cut-up arm or my knees, so I show him, and then I go inside.

Ivy is sitting at the table with a pile of beet greens she is picking over.

"That's not enough for dinner," I tell her, and she jumps a little when she hears me.

"Mirabel," she yells. "Charlie *Aaaa-aaaanne* is back."

Then she laughs and tells me I'm going to get the what-for because I've been gone so long.

Mirabel is rolling biscuits. Her eyes burn the floor under my feet.

"I've been calling you all afternoon, Charlie Anne. Where have you been?" Her face is red and puffy from the heat.

Mirabel cuts the biscuits with a jelly jar. No one's said anything about my knees. I sit in the rocking chair and start rocking. Birdie comes over and stands beside me, sticking out her hand.

"Want a lick?"

I look at the lemon drop that is now thin enough to see through.

"No, Birdie. This is not the time for lemon drops." Then she tries to climb on my lap.

"Birdie, can't you see I'm too sore?" I point to my knees.

"I don't want to be rocked. I just want to come over. What's wrong with that?"

"What happened to you?" asks Mirabel. She reaches for the jug of vinegar and pours some on a cloth and then rubs my knees. "Here, hold it there," she says, and then I start whimpering from the sting of all that vinegar.

"Why do you have to make a to-do about absolutely everything, Charlie Anne?"

I tell her how I fell off my swing, and before I can get ahold of my tongue, I tell her that the new Mrs. Jolly got here and how I met her and everything. I leave Phoebe out of it.

"That so?" says Mirabel, taking the cloth and dabbing my knee, and I cry out. Then she tells me I should have thought about doing my chores instead of swinging and that now I have to go to bed without any supper. I tell her I can't do that because I didn't have any lunch. I should have thought about that before I ran off, she says.

Then she puts the vinegar away and slides the biscuits into the oven and tells me I'll have plenty more chores tomorrow to make up for the ones I didn't do today. I catch Ivy making faces at me, and then I walk up to the attic and lie down on my bed and listen to my bed humming that happy tune, trying to make me feel better. I tell my belly that after it had so many doughnuts, it cannot be as hungry as it thinks it is.

I 2

"Go get the long-handle shovel from the barn," Mirabel tells me while I am plowing through my second bowl of oatmeal. "I want you to muck under the privy."

"Oh, that's Papa's job," I tell her, reaching for more strawberries to pile on top.

Ivy looks up, all interested. She hasn't been eating her oatmeal at all, just pushing it around the bottom of her bowl. I give her my stop-playing-with-your-food look and she gives me her mind-your-own-business look. "Didn't Papa say that was your job now, Charlie Anne?"

"No, Ivy, he did not." I drop my spoon so fast I make a little chip in the bowl. "I do not clean the privy. Papa does that job."

"Don't Papa me, Charlie Anne." Mirabel reaches for the bowl to look at the chip. "I want you to clean under the privy, and while you're doing that, I want you to think about how you ran off yesterday. I was just about to check the river to see if you were drowned."

"I will not. I will not do a job like that." I glare at her.

"You will," says Mirabel. "And you'll do it now. Or else."

She runs her finger over the chip and then drops the bowl into the dishpan in the sink. Next thing I know, she is sucking the blood off her finger and reaching for the vinegar jug. Birdie asks if I would like a lick of her lemon drop so I won't smell the bad smells in the privy. She pulls her sliver of candy from her pocket and hands it to me.

"You keep it, Birdie." Then I stand up and walk out of the house and let the door slam behind me. If the compost bucket were on the porch, I would kick it, just like Papa.

Belle and Anna May are lying under the butternut tree, feeling all sorry that I keep getting yelled at by Mirabel. Cows are tender-hearted like that if you don't let them get all caught up in the brier patch.

The long-handle shovel is inside the barn door, hanging next to all the other shovels and the saws, mallets and ax. Peter hangs all the tools in order, shortest to tallest. I wonder why he doesn't have to do the clean-the-privy job. How come I have to do girl chores in the house, plus the worst job on the whole farm? I grab the shovel and tell Olympia and Minnie and Bea to follow me.

Anna May wants to know what the dickens I am doing, wheeling the wheelbarrow and the shovel out to the privy on such a hot day, when maybe I would rather

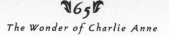

come lie under the shade of the butternut tree beside the two of them.

Humph, I say, propping up the little wooden trap-door on the back of the privy. Then I reach way down inside with my shovel and dig through the slop for a minute and pull a shovelful up, trying not to spill any on the ground because I would be sure to step in it. The holes in the bottom of Thomas's old boots are bigger than ever, and I forgot to put new cardboard inside.

I try and hold my breath the whole time I am digging. Then I step away from the privy and take many gulps of air. Already Anna May and Belle are up on their feet, wondering what that terrible smell is. I tell them, do not blame me, blame Mirabel.

I am also keeping watch for wasps. They live under the shingles on the privy and on the inside of the door and near the spot where we keep the old Sears catalog.

It takes me a long, long time to fill the wheelbarrow, partly because the job is so hard and partly because Olympia and Minnie and Bea keep trying to get down there.

My head gets all dizzy from holding my breath so much, and I smack the side of the privy with my full shovel, dropping a load of muck on the ground and sending a swarm of wasps into the air.

Oh, no, says Anna May.

Oh, no, says Belle.

I rush out of the way, stepping in the muck, and then I have to go rest for a while with Anna May and Belle, at least until things calm down with the wasps. I tell them how the privy smell is the worst smell on the farm. Cow manure and horse manure and pig manure and even chicken manure are small potatoes compared to the smell that comes from a privy.

"Ghastly," I say.

Terrible, says Anna May.

The worst, Belle agrees.

Pretty soon Mirabel comes out on the porch and sees me resting next to Anna May and Belle. She puts her hands on her hips and turns her face into one big frown.

I don't want to go to bed hungry again, so I hurry and push the wheelbarrow off to the woods. I think the stink is getting into my cuts and making them hurt even worse.

Ivy is sitting out on the fence pulling a daisy apart, petal by petal, and throwing them at me. "What's that terrrrrible smell, Charlie Anne? Oh, it's yooouuuuuu!"

I make a beeline for her, waving my shovel, chasing her all the way up through the yard and straight through the blankets hanging on the line, and when she gets all tangled up and falls down, pulling the clean blankets with her, I hurry up and go back to the privy before Mirabel thinks it's all my fault.

Anna May and Belle are looking at me like maybe I should not have done that, like I'm really going to get the what-for now, and that's when I hear someone squealing over at Old Mr. Jolly's house. I prop my shovel against the privy and walk down past the blackberries and the barn and the grapevines and the stone wall, and the whole time I am noticing how everything still smells like I am standing in muck. I sniff under my arms and along the inside of my elbows, and when I look up, that's when I see it is Phoebe who is screeching, Phoebe who is soaring through the sky on a swing like I have never seen before.

I watch without breathing as she pulls the swing into the barn and then comes shooting out, fast as a bullet, screaming the whole way. She sticks her legs straight out in front of her and sweeps one arm way out to the side and bends over backward, as if she's about to back-flip. She sees me and I wave to her and my feet start telling me they just about cannot stand the wait anymore. Don't worry about Mirabel one bit, they tell me, and what's taking so long, anyway, and hurry up.

"Want to try?" she asks when I get across the road, and I nod yes, yes, I surely do.

"I'll show you how to do it," and she soars back into the barn. Then she makes me stand and watch her for about a hundred minutes to see how fine the swing is and how good she is at swinging, and how to swing just like she does.

Then she waves for me to come into the barn so I can see how she climbs up to the loft (I know all about haylofts) and how she jumps onto the sitting board (I know all about jumping up like that) and how she takes off and soars out of the barn. Then she comes back and lands on a special platform that Old Mr. Jolly must have built for her.

"See? That's how you do it."

I hurry up the ladder. "I know how to swing," I tell her.

"Well, I want you to watch one more time." She laughs and jumps on the swing again and flies outside.

A frown as big as Mirabel's forms on my face. Then Phoebe is back. "Did you watch?"

"Phoebe," I say, my voice a little hard from the weight of my frown, "I know how to swing."

"Well, we'll see," she says, handing me the rope.

I grab it, and just the weight of it feels good in my hands.

"That's right," says Phoebe, stepping close to help. "Yes, that's good. Now hold on here—"

"Will you stop it?" I can't help myself. "I KNOW HOW TO RIDE ON A . . ."

I stop because Phoebe is holding her nose. "What's that awful smell, Charlie Anne?"

"Oh," I say, backing down a little, remembering the privy and my boots with the holes in the bottom and how I stepped in the muck lots of times. And then Phoebe is saying, "You can't go on my swing smelling like that, Charlie Anne," and I am backing up, backing down, rushing down that ladder, and the last thing I see is Phoebe with her face all puckered up.

"I don't want to ride on her stupid swing anyway," I tell Anna May and Belle as I rush across the road, my eyes already filling with tears.

Their eyes fill with cow-sorrow. They tell me they wouldn't want to ride on Phoebe's swing, either.

Mirabel shoos me right back outside. "Don't come in here until you've gotten rid of every bit of that smell." She hands me soap and tells me to go for a swim in the river. "And bring Birdie."

We take off our clothes and jump in the cold water, watching the whole time for the oldest Thatcher boy because sometimes he spies on us.

While we are swimming, I tell Birdie about Phoebe's new swing and about how it can go higher than I've ever seen a swing go before.

"Do you think she can see Mama in heaven when she swings so high?" asks Birdie, who is floating on her back as I scrub her hair.

"Probably," I say, and the thought of that, that Phoebe has a swing so high she can probably see our mama, makes me feel worse than anything.

13

Mirabel tells me I can make up for my bad behavior by making a vinegar pie to welcome our new neighbor like the good Lord intended.

"I will take the pie over and give it to Mrs. Jolly," Mirabel is telling me, "and you can go, too, Charlie Anne, if you make it especially good, with a high fluted crust and brown sugar sprinkled on top."

Mirabel is hanging sheets on the line. She is making me hand her clothespins and watch how she spreads the sheets out just right so they don't dry with wrinkles.

Mirabel flaps a sheet in front of her. "It's very important because no one wants to sleep in a mussed bed." I look over at Belle and Anna May. They could care less about sheets. I roll my eyes.

I measure out the flour and the salt and mix the lard in with a fork until everything looks like little peas. I add enough water until it balls up like a good crust should, then sprinkle flour on the table and roll the whole thing out so it fits the pan.

I am wondering all about Rosalyn and what did she want to come live with Old Mr. Jolly for, when he can't take care of a cow as fine as Belle, and about Phoebe, and how I don't want to see her at all after she clothespinned her nose. But I do wonder what happened to her mama, and why does she want to be a maid, anyway. She must hate chores as much as I do. Mostly, I would like some more of those doughnuts.

While the pie is baking, I pull a bucket of water from the well and give my dress a scrubbing right there beside the porch. The water is so cold that my fingers want to know what I am doing, but I keep rubbing my dress with Mirabel's no-children-allowed special lavender soap until the stains start disappearing. Then I wring it out as best I can and put it back on, sniffing myself one more time, just to make sure.

"What's the matter with it?" Old Mr. Jolly is saying when we are standing up on his porch, just about to knock.

"It's a little, well, plain. Wouldn't you say?"

"It's suited me fine all these years, Rosalyn."

"Well, I think just a little paint would brighten it up. Maybe some yellow."

"I don't have money for paint, Rosalyn."

"You know I have a little."

Old Mr. Jolly lets out a long sigh, which we can hear clear as cowbells. "I'm a proud man, Rosalyn. I don't want to be using your money."

"Pride isn't going to get me new paint, now, is it?"

We hear grumbling and Old Mr. Jolly's low voice: "Do what you want, Rosalyn." Then the porch door flies open and nearly hits us. He frowns when he sees us, and he hurries straight to the barn. I wonder if he has a think-about-it chair out there, right beside Phoebe's beautiful new swing.

"Yoo-hoo," says Mirabel. "Yoo-hoo."

This brings Rosalyn and Phoebe right out. "Charlie Anne, I was just wondering about all those cuts of yours," Rosalyn says. "How are you?"

"She's fine, just fine," says Mirabel, looking at Rosalyn's trousers, which are yellow as sunflowers, and then at Phoebe's, which are lavender. Phoebe smiles, but Mirabel ignores her and turns to Rosalyn.

"Charlie Anne told me we had a new neighbor and I wanted to have a proper introduction," she says. "I'm Mirabel, the cousin of this child's mother, rest her soul." She holds the pie out to Rosalyn.

"Why, it's beautiful, such a stunning pie!" Rosalyn takes it and puts it on the table and we all go over and look at it for a minute, even Phoebe. I am wondering if Mirabel will tell Rosalyn that I am the one who made the pie, but she does not.

I wonder if Phoebe will let me ride on the swing when we are done looking at the pie. I give myself a little extra sniff to be sure I still smell okay. I think maybe

Phoebe notices. I tell my face it better not turn all red. Then I move closer to Mirabel.

"Yes," she is saying, looking at the pie. "I came right after the funeral. It was just about a year ago now. I took one look at the condition of those children, and that was that. I've been here ever since. My cousin Sylvie was just the sweetest thing, but she left the children not knowing much about the way the world works. Especially this one here."

Rosalyn has already raised an eyebrow. I am backing away from Mirabel. Rosalyn looks at me and smiles. "She looks quite fine to me."

"Yes, it's manners and acting like a proper young lady and all those things that country children who don't go to school have so much trouble with. And chores. They all have a great deal of trouble getting anything done."

Rosalyn is raising her other eyebrow. "Did you say no school?"

"Yes, ever since that teacher left for California, we've been without. And she wasn't here for a year, and there were years between this one and the last. We've had trouble finding teachers who are willing to come this far out."

"Is that so?" Rosalyn is looking over at Phoebe and smiling just the tiniest bit.

Mirabel nods toward Phoebe and looks back at

Rosalyn. "Nice you brought a maid and all." Mirabel is looking at Phoebe's trousers. "None of us can afford help up here. Times are too tough. We do what we can, though."

Phoebe looks at Rosalyn, and then I see Phoebe stiffen up like she has an old ironing board down the back of her shirt. A big long shadow passes over Rosalyn's face.

Rosalyn must have brought a whole shipload of books, because there are stacks of them everywhere. Old Mr. Jolly should get busy right away building bookshelves, just as soon as he does something about that brier patch. I am counting all the books while I wait for Rosalyn's shadow to pass.

Mirabel is looking around for a place to sit, but Rosalyn does not tell her to please sit and take a weight off your feet the way folks usually do around here. So we just stand feeling all uncomfortable. This gets Mirabel's mouth running again.

"The Ellis family had colored help once a while back," Mirabel is telling Rosalyn. "They didn't last, though. Soon as times started getting hard, the help up and left, off to Ohio so I hear, and no one has heard a stitch from them since." Mirabel does not even take a breath. My ears start burning, they are feeling so uncomfortable being here with Mirabel.

"Phoebe is not my maid," Rosalyn says finally.

Mirabel looks all confused. "No?"

"No," says Rosalyn, putting her arm around Phoebe.

Mirabel is turning red. "Well, what is she, then? She's colored."

"Aah," says Rosalyn, glancing down at Phoebe and squeezing her again. "I hadn't noticed." Then she walks over to the table, picks up the pie, carries it back and puts it in Mirabel's hands.

14

Mirabel marches me home so fast I can hear her leather shoes snapping.

"I don't want you over there again," she says from about five steps ahead. "I certainly don't want you near that colored girl."

She stomps up the porch steps and puts the pie on the kitchen table and tells all of us that she is going to sit right down right now and write another letter to Eleanor and how if any of us know what is good for us, we will get out and hoe all those potatoes before she counts ten. "Here, take this pie with you."

"We do not need Aunt Eleanor," I tell her, taking the pie, and she does not even bother to look up because she is already sitting down writing. "YOU ARE NOT RAISING US," I tell her.

That gets Mirabel to look at me. "Charlie Anne, it's like you don't listen to a thing I've been trying to teach you."

Birdie comes over and takes my hand and tries to pull me away. She does not like yelling. But I have some things to say.

"We do not need you," I tell Mirabel.

I decide I need to drop the pie all over her clean floor and that is what I do. While she's screaming her head off, I grab Birdie's hand and shoo everyone out the door.

"You've really done it this time, Charlie Anne," says Ivy.

When we are out hoeing, Becky Ellis walks up by the edge of our fence. I tell her to come and help rather than just standing there looking all stupid at us.

"Charlie Anne, you are rotten to the core." Then she throws the apple she is eating and it lands at my feet.

"Charlie Anne, we are getting the electric as soon as those wires go up, and you're not!" she yells. "That's right, Charlie Anne. My mother says only some families are getting lights, and you are not one of them. You and the Morrells are too poor to have electric. You'll be using kerosene your whole life."

Papa used to say that the Morrell family had it worse than anyone else in town. That is why Mr. Morrell was the first to sign up to go build roads up north. That is also why he took three of his boys with him. That left their mama with only three little girls to feed. I see the Morrell girls at church, and they have not had new shoes for even longer than me. Becky Ellis says they do not even have underpants under their dresses.

I pick up the apple core Becky just threw at me and fling it back at her. "You better get off your high-and-mighty!"

"Stop," says Ivy, who is rushing toward me. "Will you just shut up, Charlie Anne?"

"What are you talking about, Ivy? Did you hear what she just said?"

Ivy rolls her eyes at me and throws down her hoe. She hurries toward Becky.

"You never used to be like this!" I yell after her. "Before Mama died, you would never try and be friends with someone like BECKY ELLIS."

It is sickening. Becky might let Ivy shine her sweet pretty shoes, and Ivy will be stupid enough to do it. I watch Ivy walk up to Becky. They deserve each other.

The rest of us hoe for a few minutes, and I tell them if Ivy is not helping, then we're not working, either. Maybe we could take a break and play some hide-and-seek in the cornfield until she comes back.

Mirabel does not want us in the cornfield because we might break the corn. I tell Birdie and Peter to be very careful and that I will count first. "Now scat."

They run into the corn and I start counting and then I say ready or not and when I look up, Phoebe is looking at me.

We are both quiet for a minute, me looking at

Phoebe, and Phoebe looking at me. I wonder what she is thinking. I look down at my bare feet. Ever so slightly I try and sniff at myself.

"Hi," she says.

"Hi," I say. "I heard you swinging."

"Joseph fixed it so it will go even higher."

"Joseph?" I say, looking up to the field on the other side of the barn, where all of a sudden Anna May starts bellowing her head off.

"My new father," she explains.

"Old Mr. Jolly is your new father? I thought you were just there helping them." I look at Phoebe and I am a little confused and she is looking at me the way I look at my chickens when they forget who belongs to the eggs and who does not.

"I am not the maid," says Phoebe softly.

"I knew that," I say, looking back to see what is bothering Anna May. "It was Mirabel who thought that."

Phoebe just stands there watching me until Anna May starts bellowing again, and I drop the hoe and run to see what the dickens is wrong with my cow.

I can hardly believe it. There is Old Mr. Jolly putting a rope around Belle's neck and trying to take her back to his field.

Belle is standing in the field right up next to Anna May and she has her legs stiff as a board and her feet are deep in the mud from where it rained last night.

"What are you doing?" I say, reaching him in about two seconds. "You leave her alone." As soon as Belle hears me, she starts mooing and hollering, and Old Mr. Jolly starts looking all kinds of furious.

"What have you done with my cow, Charlie Anne?" he asks, softening his voice as soon as he sees Phoebe standing right beside me.

"What do you mean, what have I done with your cow? I have not done a single cotton thing to your cow."

"It's like you've got her brainwashed or something." Old Mr. Jolly is pulling on Belle, and when she does nothing but look all sorry-like over at Anna May, Old Mr. Jolly goes around to her backside and gives her a push.

"That doesn't work," I tell him.

Old Mr. Jolly gives her another shove.

"She likes it better here. That's why she stays. What do you mean by going off and leaving her and everything without anyone watching over her so she could get all caught up in those briers, anyway?"

"He went to get me," says Phoebe. "And Rosalyn."

Old Mr. Jolly stops pushing and turns to both of us. "The Thatcher boy was supposed to be taking care of her, Charlie Anne."

"Well, you should have asked me. That Thatcher boy doesn't know how to care about anything."

I go around and whisper in Belle's ear that she better get herself out of the mud pretty soon or she'll be stuck so deep I won't be able to help her, and then before I can say milk cow, she is out of the mud and running over to Anna May, and then the two of them turn and head for the butternut tree.

"Maybe that cow needs to be with her mama," Phoebe says.

"Humph," says Old Mr. Jolly as we watch my cows go up the hill. He opens his mouth to say something else, but then he closes it again.

"You should have asked me to take care of her," I say, just before Old Mr. Jolly turns and heads home without another word. "I know how to take care of cows."

"Thank you for saying that, about Belle needing her mama," I say, pleased to see my cows munching under the butternut tree, and remembering that Peter and

Birdie are still hiding all this time. "Want to play hide-and-seek with us?"

Phoebe says yes she does want to play with us and I say okay do you want me to count all over again and she says no she can hide pretty fast.

So I turn around and see how Ivy is now up in the tree picking sour apples and throwing them down to Becky. Becky keeps dropping them and letting them stay where they fall and telling Ivy to watch better where she is throwing. Then I turn around and go looking in the corn.

I find Birdie first because she is a terrible hider. She does not understand how you have to do more than just pretend people cannot see you. "I found you, Birdie," I whisper as soon as I walk up to her, and she laughs. She's been waiting so long for me that she's pulled a corn husk and is making it into a doll. Mama taught me how to do that and I showed Birdie and now she makes little corn-husk girls all the time.

I find Phoebe lying on the ground between two rows of corn. Her trousers give her away. Then Phoebe and Birdie come help me find Peter.

We run all the way to the end of the field, almost to the river and so close to Mama I can hear her laughing she is so happy to see us, and when we get to the end of the corn, there is Peter sitting on the fence.

"It took you about forever," he says. "Where've you

been?" Then he sees Phoebe, and he stares at her for so long that I have to finally go over and kick a little sense into him, and then he says, "Hey."

I tell Peter this is Phoebe and Phoebe this is Peter and then Peter stares kind of stupid at Phoebe for a minute so I have to pinch some manners into him, the good kind (you do not stare at people and make them feel all uncomfortable) and then we all go up by Mama and I say Mama this is Phoebe and Phoebe this is Mama and Mama says she is so happy to meet Phoebe.

"Pleased to meet you, ma'am," says Phoebe, and Mama says why don't we all sit for a spell, and we do. The river is rushing this morning after all the rain.

"Charlie Anne, do you remember what Mama looked like?" Peter whispers so only I can hear.

"She has red hair," I whisper. "Do you remember her dress with all the strawberries that are the same color as her hair, and her freckles? Do you remember all her freckles?"

Peter is shaking his head. "I don't remember too much, Charlie Anne," and then I notice his eyes are getting wet, and I reach over and pull him closer to me.

"Maybe if I keep being sad, I won't forget her anymore," he whispers.

While I am thinking about this, about how people who die can disappear more every day, Birdie reaches over and touches the skin on Phoebe's face. Birdie is like that. She does not know about how sometimes maybe you should not be touching someone's face. We watch Birdie scrape up some dirt and then rub her doll's face until it is dark as Phoebe. Birdie holds the doll to her heart.

I hope Phoebe knows Birdie does not mean anything bad by the things she does. I guess maybe she does understand because Birdie goes over and climbs on Phoebe's lap and Phoebe lets her stay there.

When we are down by the corn, we see the oldest Thatcher boy shooting his gun at crows in the big white pines by the river. We rush back inside to hide between the stalks. "That Thatcher boy is a snake," I whisper to Phoebe. "You stay away."

"What's so bad about him?" she whispers back.

So I tell her my Thatcher story: "Well, his papa got killed in a hunting accident. And ever since then, the mama has been mean and the dogs have been meaner and the oldest boy is the meanest of all."

Finally, when we come out of the corn and are back at the potatoes, there is Ivy, standing and looking at us, her face all red.

"I watched you," says Ivy. "I watched you playing with that colored girl." She points at Phoebe.

"Shut up, Ivy." I move in front of Phoebe.

"I'm telling Mirabel." Ivy runs off toward home, and

even though her legs are longer than mine, I am faster, and when I catch her, I give her a big shove and she falls into the dirt.

I pick up a big handful of mud. "If you tell," I say, giving her my most terrible mad face, "I will make you eat this."

"If you don't let me up, I'm going to tell on you right now. Now let me up."

"You better let her up, Charlie Anne," says Peter. "You don't want to miss supper again, do you?"

"I don't care," I tell Peter, but I let Ivy up.

"Becky told me to watch out for coloreds and now we have one on our own land," Ivy says as soon as she is standing.

Then Becky comes up beside us with a big ugly grin on her face. "Whoever heard of a girl wearing trousers like that," she says, pointing at Phoebe. "What's the matter, you want to be a boy?"

"I'm not a boy," Phoebe says softly, looking a little smaller all of a sudden. Birdie reaches for Phoebe's hand. She pulls the lemon drop out of her pocket with her other hand and offers it to Phoebe.

"Don't you dare!" shrieks Ivy. "Don't you dare eat our candy." Phoebe just gives Ivy a mad look and takes the candy and pops it in her mouth.

"I'm telling. I'm telling you let a colored girl eat off your lemon drop."

Then I push Ivy good and hard. She stumbles in the

dirt again, and this time she is crying that I broke her nose, and Becky Ellis is laughing. Ivy gives Becky a why-are-you-laughing-at-me look. Becky shrugs and runs off toward her house.

"Good riddance," says Peter, looking shyly over at Phoebe.

"God ribbons," says Birdie.

I cannot help grinning just the tiniest bit at what Birdie says and Phoebe sees me and then I see the corner of her mouth start lifting up and then we look straight at each other and tell each other with just our eyes that we should not burst out laughing right now because it might hurt Birdie's feelings.

"You broke my nose," Ivy is still saying, and then she gets up and rushes off to Mirabel, and I know it won't be long before I get the what-for.

Ivy is sitting on the table, with a big towel on her head, her face tilted back to stop the bleeding, and Mirabel is reaching for the vinegar jug. The letter to Aunt Eleanor is sealed and sitting on the table ready for the post.

"I told. I told on you, Charlie Anne."

"Up to bed this instant," says Mirabel as soon as she sees me.

"Why?" I say, glaring at Ivy.

"Thank God her nose isn't broken, that's all I've got

to say. And what's this I hear about you playing with that colored girl? Now listen up good, Charlie Anne. You are not to play with that girl. People will talk. Do you understand?"

"About what? Why will people talk?"

"Young lady, you've never even been out of this town. You don't know what the world is like. Heavens, if you had your way, you'd be associating with coloreds all the time. Have you no sense?"

I look at her hard and I keep my mouth clamped shut and then I march right past her and up to my bed.

We'll just see about that.

Mirabel means what she says. She does not let me near Phoebe. Instead, I get more manners lessons than ever.

Mirabel sits in Mama's rocking chair in the parlor each night when the supper dishes are done and pulls out *The Charm of Fine Manners* and makes Ivy and me and Birdie crowd around her on the floor. We are supposed to keep busy while we are listening, so tonight there is a big bowl of onions on the floor for us to peel for creamed onions tomorrow.

"How come Peter doesn't have to do this?" I want to know, big onion tears rolling down my cheeks. "How come he gets to go out to the barn?"

"He does not need to learn to grow up to be the mistress of a home. You do, Charlie Anne. All young ladies need to know how to cream onions."

Ivy snickers and I throw an onion at her and she screeches and Mirabel has to put down her book and tell me if I don't start behaving myself, I will be here all night peeling onions, and then she picks up the book and starts again:

> One great reason why so many
> fail of making any success in life

is that they have not the power of
sticking steadily to their work.

❧

Mirabel looks up from the book and down over her
reading glasses and she gives me her I-told-you-so look.
Then she starts again:

> They get tired, and want to stop;
> whereas the true worker works
> though he is tired—works till it
> doesn't tire him to work; works
> on, unheeding the numerous
> temptations to turn aside to this
> or that diversion.

❧

I wipe my eyes with Mama's old apron and reach for
another onion.

We begin having wash day Mondays and ironing Tues-
days and house-sweeping and rug-beating Wednesdays,
and Thursdays and Fridays are for canning and putting
up vegetables and baking. Every day is gardening day.

I am hoeing carrots with Birdie. She keeps licking
off her lemon drop and putting it back in her pocket
and then picking up the hoe, but the wood handle
keeps sticking to her hand, and even worse than that, a
yellow jacket has noticed the lemon drop, too, and is
circling around her face.

"Make it go away, make it go away, Charlie Anne." She is crying and screaming to make it go away, but the bee keeps coming closer, closer, and Anna May and Belle are up on their feet now, moving closer to us, wondering why the dickens I don't do something about that yellow jacket.

The bee lands on the thin skin between Birdie's thumb and first finger and holds on, all interested in the smell of her lemon drop, and I swat at it, but it keeps holding on, and then before I can say cow pie, Birdie is howling.

This is what you do to help Birdie forget her bee sting.

"How about a chicken race?"

She is sucking on her finger. Tears are sliding down her cheeks. I am making a mud bandage by spitting into a bit of dirt. "It is much better than vinegar." I dab it on the bee sting. "See?"

She nods and says, "Mirabel gets really mad when we have chicken races, Charlie Anne."

"She's organizing all those canning jars in the basement. She won't even know. Come on. Let's go find Minnie and Olympia and Bea."

You would think our chickens would stay close to the barn, but they can be anywhere: up by the porch, down by the privy, out by the garden, pecking around the compost. Today we find them out by the blackberry bushes.

I let Birdie have first pick, on account of her bee sting and all, plus I know she will pick Minnie. Birdie doesn't understand that maybe you shouldn't be choosing a plump little chicken that lets you cuddle her. I myself go for Olympia, who is tall and lean, because I want a chicken that can win.

Setting up a chicken race is pretty easy, actually. You need a start line (Birdie's hoe) and a finish line (my hoe) and two chickens that you hold on to, patting gently, until you say ready set go, and then you're allowed one little push, and that's all.

From then on, all you can do is holler. No touching.

"All right, Birdie?"

She nods. She is whispering to Minnie and stroking her head.

"Ready. Set. Go!" I give Olympia a little push and she squawks and rushes ahead. Birdie taps Minnie on the bottom. Anna May and Belle come up by the fence because if there's one thing about cows, they love a good chicken race.

"Go!" I scream. "Move your butt, Olympia. Gooooooooo."

Everything is fair in a chicken race, so when Olympia decides to stop and peck at a june bug, I have to let her. Meanwhile, Birdie has moved around to the finish line and is calling "Here, chick. Here, chick" in that soft voice of hers, and wouldn't you know it, there is Minnie scurrying toward the finish line.

There are no walls to keep our chickens on the race-course, so when Olympia heads for a quick escape, I rush right over and stand in front of her. "Shoo," I say, trying to herd her back toward the finish line. "Shoo."

I hear Anna May and Belle cheering for Minnie. "Be quiet," I tell them.

As Minnie crosses the finish line, Phoebe comes hurrying over.

"You can have Olympia," I tell her.

"No, Charlie Anne. I want the other one."

So then we have to go back down by the blackberry bushes and find Bea and bring her up and start the whole race over again.

"Move your big butt, Olympiaaaaa!" I scream. "Goooooooooo."

Anna May and Belle stop cheering, and all of a sudden their faces fill with cow-worry and then they are telling me oh no, oh no, here comes Mirabel, but I am so busy shooing Olympia over the finish line that I can't take even a second to look up.

This time, Mirabel's frown is big as the barn. She takes a long icy look at Phoebe. "Go home," she says. "You're not wanted here."

"Mirabel, it wasn't her fault," I say, shooing Olympia away from my feet. "It was my idea to have the

chicken race because of Birdie's bee sting. It's my fault we're not hoeing between the carrots."

Birdie is already holding Phoebe's hand. Mirabel steps over and slaps it away.

I see that ironing board go down Phoebe's back again. She gives Mirabel a hard look and then flies off home.

There are about one hundred ways to cook potatoes.
Mirabel knows them all: potato puff, potato casserole,
potato cream soup, potato stew, potato dodge, potato
dumplings, creamed potatoes, scalloped potatoes, potatoes with flour gravy, potato filling side dish, potato
pancakes and my favorite, pigs in a potato patch. This
is a huge pile of mashed potatoes with crisp pieces of
bacon pushed in, all over. This is Birdie's job. My job is
to peel the potatoes, lots of them.

When Mirabel was down in the cellar organizing all
the canning jars, she noticed that mice had gotten into
our potatoes from last fall.

My new job is making sure Big Pumpkin Face gets
down there every day on mouse duty. Big Pumpkin Face
is not so easy to find these days. Sometimes she is up
in the barn sunning herself, sometimes on the stone
wall sunning herself, sometimes on the porch swing—
sunning herself. She is getting fat from sunning herself
so much. "Get to work," I tell her.

While she is mousing around, I have to pick
through the bin because there's a bad smell coming
from deep inside, and when you have one rotten

potato, pretty soon you have a lot of them. We can't afford to be losing potatoes when we eat so many of them, Mirabel says. I say we could lose a few.

I begin tossing the bad ones out. Even the ones that Mirabel says we can save because they are just getting a little wrinkled, I toss into the pail, plus all the ones that have little mouse nibbles on them. Then I carry the whole load out to the compost pile.

Phoebe and Rosalyn are out by the road working in their garden. Anna May and Belle want to know why don't I take a little stroll over to see them, and I tell them I think I will. I throw down the potato pail.

They are planting seeds and humming. I hear their fence being all happy about their company.

"What are you planting?"

"Sunflowers," says Phoebe. "Want to help?"

"Sunflowers, by the road? Most people plant them by their gardens. Sunflowers are for birds."

"That may be so," says Rosalyn, standing up and wiping the sweat off her face, "but I want people who walk by here to know there's a family living here now. And these are the only seeds I have."

Rosalyn hands me a shovel. "Here, why don't you help us plant some of these seeds. Do you know how?"

Do I know how to plant seeds? I roll my eyes.

After I am digging for a while, I say, "My mama used to plant flowers with me."

"Yes," says Rosalyn. "I'm sorry you've lost your mother, Charlie Anne."

"Yes," I say, because when you think about it, what else is there to say?

"Would you like to come in with us and have some sweet raspberry tea?" Rosalyn wants to know.

I don't even pause. "Yes," I say, because when you think about it, what else is there to really say.

There are big changes happening inside Old Mr. Jolly's house. Everything is getting painted and made over. Someone has even touched up the roses on the wallpaper so they are blooming again.

The stairs going up to Phoebe's room are the color of the sky on a good day. Rosalyn has made new covers for the sofa and chairs, so now everything is dressed up in her trouser cloth: red pepper red, crushed blueberry, sunflower yellow, evergreen.

Phoebe has made curtains out of muslin sheets, and she's embroidered little cornflowers and poppies along the hems. Old Mr. Jolly has been busy making bookshelves, and now the one thousand books that Rosalyn brought are neatly tucked in together, and everything smells good, too, because there are dishes of cinnamon and cloves and nutmeg on the shelves.

Just like at our house, there is no electricity, but there is a kerosene lamp on the kitchen table. And when Rosalyn pours us all cups of sweet raspberry tea, I am noticing we are all glowing with a special light. Even Old Mr. Jolly.

18

For about the hundredth time, I want to see Phoebe's bedroom way up under the eaves, but she keeps telling me no, she has never had a room to herself and it is not ready for visitors, but soon, soon, soon.

What does it look like? I want to know. I am imagining it must feel like a castle to have a room all your own.

"It's a surprise. You'll see."

"Today?" I ask as soon as I see her the next day.

"No," she says, her hands covered with whitewash. "Maybe tomorrow."

"Today?" I ask when I see her the next day.

"No. Maybe tomorrow."

"That's what you said yesterday."

"Come on," she says, laughing at my pouting face. "You can help me pick these flowers."

"What's it like?" I ask as we walk through Old Mr. Jolly's fields, picking black-eyed Susans and goldenrod and wild asters and rose hips.

Phoebe smiles. "You'll see. Soon."

The briers are cleaned out. Any day now, Old Mr. Jolly will come looking for Belle. I sigh and pick a clump of daisies.

"I will light a candle in my window when I am ready," Phoebe says. "Make sure you watch for it."

That night, there is a candle burning in Phoebe's window. I light one, too, to say yes, I'll be there, but your room better be ready, because I'm getting awful sick of the waiting.

It takes forever to get Anna May milked and two eggs found and then Ivy burns the oatmeal so I have to help her start over and show her how to do things. "Don't you know anything?" I tell her, and she starts screeching, "Mirabel! Charlie Anne is being mean to meeeeeeee!"

"What are you rushing for?" Mirabel wants to know, and Ivy says, "Yes, what are you up to, Charlie Anne?"

I want to get over to see Phoebe so badly, but I still have to wash the dishes and put everything away and finally, finally, I rush outside, not bothering to listen if Mirabel is going to give me any more work. I am too excited about Phoebe's new room.

I rush across the street and right up on their porch and I plow into Old Mr. Jolly and he says what the heck, what the heck, and before he can say anything to me about Belle I fly in the house. I bump into Rosalyn and she points up those sky blue steps and before you can count ten I am sprinting up and they are steeper even than my stairs and they creak with every step and then I turn the corner and finally, finally, I see Phoebe's room.

She is standing in the doorway. "Welcome, Charlie Anne."

The walls are whitewashed and the trim is that same happy sky color and the bed has a bedspread made with the sunflower trousers cloth. There are curtains at the little windows under the eaves with little roses embroidered on them and the floor has been oiled and shines in the sun that is pouring through the window.

There is a washstand with a pitcher and bowl for washing her hands and face and a table beside her bed that has a little white cloth and on top are several books.

She shows me her closet, where her trousers are hanging in a neat row beside some dresses, and she points to a secret door that Old Mr. Jolly has made.

We go inside and there is a blanket on the floor and a secret window that looks outside and I see Ivy carrying the compost bucket out to the garden.

"Tell me a secret you never told anyone else," Phoebe is saying.

I feel a little nervous. I never shared secrets before with anyone but Mama. "You first," I tell her.

"Okay." She closes her eyes and thinks for a while. I watch Ivy dump the compost and bring the bucket back up to the porch. Then she looks over at Old Mr. Jolly's house and I move away from the window.

Phoebe opens her eyes. "My mama told me there was a light inside me that no one could put out unless I let them."

I lean back against the rafters and breathe in the warm smell of the old timbers. I think about what she said. "That's a good secret."

"Now tell me."

I look at her. I hope I can trust her. I close my eyes, and begin. "Sometimes my mama talks to me, usually when I am up by the river near her grave, but other times, too. Sometimes I think I hear her just before I wake up."

When I open my eyes, Phoebe is smiling. "That's a good secret, too," she says.

Then Rosalyn is calling us down to lunch. While we are slurping the best vegetable soup I ever had, Rosalyn says, "Maybe Charlie Anne would like to hear *David Copperfield?*" and Phoebe goes over to the one thousand books and brings one back to the table and starts to read.

Well. Phoebe reads way better than me and pretty soon I forget all about where I am and how Mirabel is probably looking for me by now. I want to know how Phoebe learned to read so good, when I can't hardly read at all, but I am too caught up in the story to stop her and ask.

"Would you like a turn?" asks Rosalyn, pushing the book toward me. I am shaking my head no, no, no, and that's when I hear Mirabel down by the road calling me, and for the first time ever, I am glad. I won't have to watch the letters all jumble and remember all about Miss Moran if I get away from Rosalyn and Phoebe quick enough. Which I do.

19

Mirabel tells us we are going to start going to church, and this means Saturdays are bath day, and this means about a hundred trips to the well to get the water that we need to fill the washtub that we pull to the middle of the kitchen floor.

We hang a curtain from the ceiling, but you really don't get any privacy at all. "Get out of here," I tell Birdie, who keeps wandering in when it is my turn.

Mirabel comes in with the dress I wore to Mama's funeral.

"I am not wearing that dress," I tell her, feeling that awful hole inside me that opens up any time I look at that dress, and Mirabel says, "Yes, you are, because tomorrow your aunt Eleanor is coming."

She pulls an envelope from the front of her apron and slaps it down on the table.

"Papa said not Aunt Eleanor."

"Don't Papa me," Mirabel says, holding a towel up for me.

"I can do it myself," I say, snapping the towel out of her hands and holding it in front of me.

Birdie is already naked as a baby jaybird, and as soon

as I'm out, Mirabel lifts her up and plunks her in. Mirabel starts scrubbing Birdie's arms with a washrag. "And, Charlie Anne, I want you to make two of those vinegar pies, one for church and one for when Eleanor comes."

I pick up the letter and open it and try to read it, but the letters jumble all up like they always do. Very badly I want to know what Aunt Eleanor has to say.

I look over at Ivy. She is watching me, one eyebrow raised high. "What's the matter, Charlie *Aaaa-aaaanne?*"

"Read this," I say, putting the letter in front of her.

"Why don't you, Charlie Anne? Can't you read or something?"

Ivy knows very well I can't read like she does. She knows what Miss Moran made me do. Mirabel looks over. My face is burning.

"You really can't read at all?" Mirabel asks as she scrubs Birdie's back. "I thought you were just fooling on us because you didn't like to read."

"I can read. I just have to make the pies. You give me so many chores all the time, I don't have time to practice." I pull the flour off the shelf.

Ivy is happier than I have seen her in a long while. "Does Mirabel know why Miss Moran made you stand in her trash bucket, Charlie Anne?"

That's it. I throw down the flour scoop, sending a

cloud of flour all over me and the table, and some of it even reaches Mirabel where she is trying to get the dirt off Birdie's neck. I rush at Ivy just as Mirabel starts sneezing, and I grab at Ivy's pinned curls. Ivy screams and Birdie jumps up and spills half the water all over Mirabel and all over the floor.

I don't wait to be yelled at. I run out the door and out to the butternut tree where Anna May and Belle are resting in the shade, and they want to know what was I doing in that hot kitchen when I could be so much happier sitting out here with them in the shade, watching the buttercups moving in the breeze. When I get myself settled, with my back lying all up next to Anna May and my eyes feeling all happy to be filled up with the sight of my beautiful Brown Swiss Belle, that's when the two of them tell me how very sorry they are that I am having enough troubles to fill a wheelbarrow.

"Who wants to read anyway?" I tell them.

20

The next morning is Sunday and Mirabel keeps check-ing Peter: behind his ears, his fingernails, his elbows. She gets her own comb and wets it in her coffee and slicks his hair into place. He bellows as loud as Anna May and Belle put together. Then she finishes letting out his pants, and when he puts them on, they are still so short he looks like the scarecrow Papa made to watch over his corn.

Then it is time for us to all go to church. We walk right past Old Mr. Jolly's house and Rosalyn's bright yellow new door. I look for Phoebe but there's no sign of her. Ivy is wearing the shoes she wore to Mama's funeral and she hobbles up the hill, they are so small. I am wearing Thomas's old muck boots, which I scrubbed so they don't smell and I stuffed with rags so my feet fit, and I'm not hobbling at all.

We have to walk right past the Thatchers' house, and the oldest Thatcher boy is up in a tree waiting for all the people walking to church. He throws an apple and it hits me in the arm.

"Ouch!" I scream, and I go right over and start giv-ing him a piece of my mind, how he is a snake and will always be a snake, but Mirabel takes one look at the condition of their yard, at the dogs barking and the clothesline creaking around and the paint all falling off the house, and she pulls me away.

When we get to Becky's house, Ivy pats at her curls to make sure they are sticking in place and she tries not to hobble and I think some more about how they deserve each other and then we are at church.

I put my pie on the table under the maple tree where everyone brings something to share. It is being neighborly is what we call it.

Then I go inside and tell Peter to shove over so I can sit between him and Birdie. "Even more," I tell him, because I am mighty sick of him rolling on top of me all night long. I ask Birdie where is her lemon drop, and she unrolls her balled-up hand, and I see where her skin is sticky and the lemon drop is sitting, getting thinner every day.

"Do you want a lick?"

I shake my head, and she pops it into her mouth for a minute, then spits it out into her hand and folds her fingers around it. Birdie did not want to wear her funeral dress, either, because she thinks that when she wears it, someone else will die. I take her other hand in mine and hold it and miss Mama.

We are early and so Mirabel gets to nod to the ladies

who walk in. She likes this. She is wearing her hat with gray and white feathers and a little veil that comes down on her forehead, and I cannot figure out who looks more like a mockingbird: Mirabel, or the real one that keeps flying past the Jesus picture in our stained-glass window.

The Morrell girls walk in alone, because their mother sends them without her. They are barefooted. Papa told me he thinks she is too ashamed of not having shoes.

"Why?" I asked. "That makes no sense to send them alone."

He shrugged. "Some things are just too much, that's all."

I told him I didn't see how listening to this preacher talk about the things he always talks about, how we are all terrible sinners and all, is going to do the Morrell girls or anyone else any good.

Papa laughed that day, his deep belly laugh, and he reached over and hugged me. I sigh. I miss Papa very much.

As I am thinking about Papa, Becky Ellis walks in with her mother, and they sit in their fancy pew up front, the one they donate extra money for, and Ivy places her foot right at the edge of the aisle so Becky will notice that she is wearing her fancy shoes.

Mr. and Mrs. Aldrich come in next. They are all

gray and bent over, and they can't see very well, but they always have a nice pudding cake to snack on if you ever skin your knees when you are running past their house, and they bring nice casseroles when your mama dies. Mr. Aldrich smells like nutmeg from all the baking his wife does, and Mrs. Aldrich comes right up and tousles my hair and rubs her cheek against my face, and I can smell the lavender water she washes with.

"Make sure you sing so I can hear you," says Mr. Aldrich, winking at me, and that's because I like to sing "Amazing Grace" very loud. We sing it every week.

After that, in comes Zella Polanski and her family, all pressed and polished, and then Mrs. Reilly, who I bet is wearing chicken feathers on her hat, and then Evangeline. When the church is full, there are very few men, on account of so many of them have gone up north to build roads, all except for Zella's husband and Mr. Aldrich, who are too old, and the preacher, who keeps preaching so we will one day see the light.

Then the door swings open again and in walk Rosalyn and Old Mr. Jolly and Phoebe. There is a whole lot of silence as everyone stares, because having somebody new in church doesn't happen every day and Rosalyn's hair is billowing all around her. Also, I don't think we ever had a colored girl in church before.

Old Mr. Jolly stands at the back of the church for a moment, looking like he just swallowed a pile of bad meat, and Rosalyn grabs on to Phoebe's hand and motions with her head that they should hurry and sit down. *Please.*

Old Mr. Jolly leads the way and then the whispering starts.

"So that's who he married."

"She's too young for him."

"And what are they doing bringing their maid and letting her sit with them up front like that?"

The preacher takes a good long look at Old Mr. Jolly, like he's cussing him out for being late, and then he clears his throat and begins.

You are not supposed to make people feel worse during a funeral, but that is what the preacher did at Mama's. Papa put his lips into that thin line and stopped taking us to church, even though Mama wanted us to be church-raised and all. Papa said we would let the angels guide us after that. I told him I already stopped praying after Mama had so many babies, and then went straight to heaven, and he said I did not need to worry, that angels watch over us no matter if we are mad about things or not. God is very good like that.

The preacher clears his throat, and that is my signal to look out the window and think about other things. I wonder if Phoebe is going to hate this as much as me.

2 I

Old Mr. Jolly must have told Rosalyn about how after church there is a picnic outside, because when I come out from church, she and Phoebe are already standing behind the table, taking the cover off their sharing plate.

I am stuck behind everyone, all standing and gabbing and whispering, and Zella, right in front of me, is saying to Mrs. Reilly, "She should pin her hair up or something," and Mrs. Ellis says, "Maybe he made a mistake, marrying a woman from the South, don't you think? They are funny down there."

"He's not much to look at, either; maybe she's all he could find," Zella says, laughing.

I think they sound just like Minnie and Olympia and Bea. I am trying so hard to listen to them that I do not notice what Rosalyn and Phoebe brought for sharing until I get almost right up to them.

Well. Somebody must have forgot to tell them that these are hard times and that we all bring things like vinegar pie and biscuits and jam from all the blackberries that grow around here. But no one did, because sitting on their plate are the most glorious cupcakes I have ever seen. They are chocolate with chocolate frosting so thick it looks like dark butter, just ready to be licked, and on top of each one is a little purple violet, looking up and smiling at everyone. I bet even Jesus himself is smiling, hallelujah.

"Well, will you look at those," Mrs. Ellis says, and she stops and stares for a minute, and then she skips right over them and takes one of her own sour lemon squares. When Becky reaches for a cupcake, Mrs. Ellis pushes her hand away.

"Who does she think she is?" asks Zella. "What's she doing, trying to outdo us all?"

"Somebody ought to tell her pride is a sin," laughs Mrs. Reilly.

"No thank you," Zella says with her best manners when Phoebe holds a cupcake out for her.

"No, dear," says Mrs. Reilly when it is her turn.

I notice Phoebe slump just a little. It turns out that several people hurry past Rosalyn and Phoebe's cupcakes and go right to Mirabel, who is cutting pieces of my vinegar pie, pretending it is hers.

A big long shadow moves over Rosalyn. Phoebe is about to cry. I keep trying to catch Phoebe's eye, but she is too busy trying to give her cupcakes away.

Then the little Morrell girls go up and take cupcakes from Phoebe, and then Mr. and Mrs. Aldrich take two each. I think maybe they are trying to make up for all the bad manners all around them.

When I finally get up to Phoebe, I hold out my plate. "I'll take three."

Rosalyn smiles. Phoebe looks at me all grateful-like and she piles the cupcakes on my plate. Then I tell Phoebe why doesn't she come over and sit with me by the tree, and she does. I am just itching for another invitation to her room.

"Where are your manners?" Mirabel says in her mad voice when she sees me with so many cupcakes piled on my plate, and I start wondering what the manners book will have to say about this, but before I get too far with my thinking, Mirabel reaches over and snatches one of the cupcakes and eats half of it in a single bite.

"Ohhhhh," she says, her eyes glistening. "These are won-der-ful."

Phoebe looks all proud and then Rosalyn comes over by us, and Mirabel says a quick good morning and then hurries off to find Peter.

Well. Peter is up in an old maple tree with some of his friends, and Mirabel starts yelling so loud I can hear her over here. In about one and a half seconds he is on the ground and Mirabel is marching up to us.

"We'll see them home," says Old Mr. Jolly, nodding at me and Birdie. "It will give me a chance to check on my cow."

My heart falls. Mirabel stands there considering. Phoebe looks over and squeezes my hand. "Don't worry," she whispers. "Rosalyn has already talked to him about you keeping that cow."

Finally, Mirabel nods okay, and she takes Peter by the back of his shirt and marches him off to the road. Old Mr. Jolly winks at Phoebe and bites into a cupcake and starts grinning. "Never in my life have I had anything so good," he says in a voice so loud that even the preacher looks over. I notice then that Old Mr. Jolly winks at Rosalyn.

She reaches over and hugs him and kisses him right on the lips in front of everyone—which is something we've surely never seen at church before.

"Sweet Pea?" Rosalyn says as we are walking home.

Phoebe looks up.

"Those cupcakes were delicious."

Phoebe nods.

Rosalyn reaches over and hugs her for a very long time and we all stop and watch. Then she takes one of Phoebe's hands and Old Mr. Jolly takes the other.

"One, two, three, up," says Old Mr. Jolly, and they swing Phoebe off the ground and she yelps and they set her back down and she yelps when they do it again. Just watching them, I think about my mama and how much I miss her and how my family is all broken apart.

I notice Birdie noticing, too. I reach over and take her hand and give it a little squeeze and feel what's left of her sticky lemon drop.

* * *

"We need a school," Rosalyn says as we pass Becky's house. "A school to change things. Why doesn't anyone open that school, Charlie Anne?"

I don't say anything because my heart is in my mouth and everything is going all dizzy all around me because I am remembering Miss Moran and the day she told me how the world is divided in two.

"There are those who can and those who can't," she said, stacking all the books on her desk, and pushing them away from me. "Young lady, I see now that you are someone who can't." Then she told me to sweep the floor and fill the wood box and wash the blackboard three times because it wasn't done right.

I didn't want Miss Moran to see all my tears, but I missed my mama so much my tears were a river. That was the first time Mama told me maybe it was time I started visiting her. Things would be better if I did.

22

Right away I know something's wrong. Anna May and Belle are not where they are supposed to be. They are up as close to the house as they can get. They don't like it up there. It is too close to Mirabel.

"What's going on?" Birdie is asking, and I hardly hear her because I am already flying for the house. Birdie is trying to keep up with me, yelling, "Wait, Charlie Anne, wait!" But I can't stop. I can't.

When I get close, I see what Anna May and Belle are looking at. There is Peter all packed up like a little present, his hair slick as grease, and there are Aunt Eleanor and Uncle Will beside a big black automobile in front of our house.

Peter takes one look at me and runs and tries to jump in my arms. "Noooooooooo, Charlie Anne. I don't want to go. Don't make me go with them. I don't want to go to Boston. I want to live here with you."

I look up quickly at Mirabel. "What's going on?" Peter is crying so hard, and trying to wrap his arms around me, that I lose my balance and slip and fall right into the dirt. Then Peter is on top of me, hugging me, choking me, keeping me from getting up again.

"It's for the best," says Mirabel, trying to unwrap Peter's arms from around my neck. That just makes him hold tighter.

"For the best?" I ask, choking quite a bit and trying to untangle myself. "What's for the best?"

"Mirabel is going to make me go live with them and be their little boooooooy." Then Peter sobs so hard I can feel his heart pounding right into mine. I hold on to him as tight as I can. I press my cheek against his.

Mirabel is still trying to pull Peter away from me, but he just keeps holding on. "Charlie Anne, let go," she says. Then Birdie is jumping on Peter and hugging him and squeezing herself between me and Peter and Mirabel.

"Charlie Anne, LET GO," says Mirabel.

I look up into her eyes. "NO," I tell her through the tears that have started running down my face.

"I want to go to Boston," says Ivy.

"They want a boy," says Mirabel.

"But who's going to do all the outside chores around here, if not Peter?" asks Ivy.

Mirabel looks at me and she doesn't even have to say it out loud. I know what she's thinking. Then Aunt Eleanor is beside us, trying to pull us all apart. "Charlie Anne," she says. "Are you really going to stand in the way of Peter's going to a good school and making more of himself than could ever be possible on this . . ." She looks around at our house and our barn, at Minnie and Olympia and Bea pecking in the dirt, at Anna May and Belle in the close-by field and at all of us children, and frowns. "He has a chance to better himself. Are you really going to stand in his way?"

"I don't want to go to Boston," cries Peter again, and he buries his face deeper in my arms.

Aunt Eleanor is looking at Mirabel. It looks like she is having second thoughts. "If he doesn't want to go . . . ," she says.

"Nonsense," says Mirabel. "I don't have enough food to feed them all. I haven't heard from James since he left."

Peter starts sobbing so loud that Aunt Eleanor shakes her head. "I did think he was younger. It's hard for a child this old to make a new start."

"Oh, that's ridiculous," says Mirabel. "He's only seven. Plenty young enough."

Eleanor is walking back to the car. I hold Peter tighter.

"He wants to stay with us," I tell Mirabel. "This is going to make Papa really, really mad."

This time I have the feeling I am getting through to Mirabel. She kneels down in the dirt beside Peter and tries to pull him onto her lap. Then she is whispering in his ear.

I expect she is telling him how it will be all

right, how she has changed her mind and he doesn't have to go. We will all stay here and wait for Papa and everything will be better very soon. But he starts crying even harder and I know this is not what she is telling him. Then she talks louder: "It will be all right in Boston, Peter. It is just a vacation. Just for a little while. You can go to school in Boston."

"I don't want to go to school," Peter says, and then he starts howling again.

Aunt Eleanor looks at Uncle Will. "I don't know," she says.

Uncle Will is turning a little red. He keeps looking at his watch. "I didn't come all this way," he says, finally, and then he stomps over to us and reaches down and peels Peter from my neck. He lifts him up and carries him to the big car and drops him into the backseat and slams the door.

Then Aunt Eleanor rushes to the car and climbs inside and Uncle Will starts the motor. Even before I can loosen Birdie's arms from my neck, Uncle Will is backing up out of our driveway. Peter has his face squished up against the window, and he is crying.

We all watch them go, and Birdie is sobbing because everyone else is crying, even Ivy.

I run after the big black car from Boston and rush out onto the road, and when it hurries over the hill and I can no longer see it, I start to really sob. When I look up, Anna May and Belle are looking at me all tender-hearted, and Rosalyn and Phoebe have walked across the road to see what has happened. They wrap their arms around me, and it feels very much like I am wrapped up in Mama's poppy-colored quilt. When Birdie comes over, they make room for her, too.

23

Mirabel is baking an applesauce cake to make things better. She knows I love applesauce. I know what she is up to.

"How could you?" I scream. "How could you break us apart when Mama told us family was the most important thing?"

Mirabel must see the sparks flying off my head. She puts the flour sack on the table. Birdie does not understand things like sometimes you get so mad and sad at the same time that sparks really do fly off your head when tears are rolling down your face. She rushes up and tries to pull me away from Mirabel. She does not like loud voices or tears.

"Go away, Birdie." This only makes her start crying, and then she rushes to Ivy, who is sitting at the table, waiting for supper.

"You've really done it this time," Ivy tells me, pulling Birdie up onto her lap.

Ivy never pulls Birdie up onto her lap or does anything nice for Birdie at all. I would belt her if we were alone. "Shut up, Ivy. I wish Aunt Eleanor took you, not Peter. Then we would be rid of you."

"Did you hear her?" shrieks Ivy, turning to Mirabel. "Did you hear the awful things she said to me?"

Mirabel slams her wooden spoon on the table. "Charlie Anne." She is about to say something else, but I am looking like an old boar pig ready to tear her apart, and she closes her mouth.

Birdie has given up trying to get me to stop. She is burying her face in Ivy's pinned curls.

"Look what you've done," I say, moving closer to Mirabel. "How could you send Peter away like that? He is OUR BROTHER. You made a terrible mistake. You should walk out the door and leave us and never come back, that would be the best thing you could do for us. We all hate you."

Mirabel tenses her whole body and then just stands and stares at me, her frown flat. Everyone stops crying. We are all looking at Mirabel, watching to see what she will do next.

At first, she does nothing. She just stands there looking from one of us to the other. Then she gets a little teary and turns away and looks out the window over the sink and out across our hay fields. We have never seen her eyes get even a little damp, and I have plenty of time to brace myself for what's coming next because she looks out the window for a long time. I put my hand on my chest to try and slow my speeding heart. Ivy is telling me with her eyes that I'm going to get the what-for, and I tell her with my eyes to go jump in the river.

Mirabel is good with cuts and fixing hurting fingers, and I guess she's also good at drying up her own tears, because when she turns back around, there is no trace of them.

"Charlie Anne, I saw no other way," she says. "We have not heard from your father in a long time. Anna May is hardly giving us any milk at all and those chickens are good for nothing. I got one egg yesterday. One. I wanted Eleanor to take Birdie, too, but she said no."

Well. Birdie starts screaming after that and Ivy pushes her out of her lap. Birdie comes rushing over to me and I pick her up the way I always do.

"We do not need you," I tell Mirabel. "We would be better off on our own."

"Young lady," says Mirabel, who has pulled herself almost completely back together again. "Need I keep reminding you that you are forgetting your place? I would be doing a great disservice to your mother if I let you continue to act this way toward your elders."

"Oh, why don't you just shove off?" I tell her, and then I set Birdie down on the sofa, and I don't pay any attention to her cries because I have some things I need to say to Mama.

* * *

I rush out through our corn and up on the hill where the river is churning from all the rain we got last night. I ask Mama if she knew about how Aunt Eleanor was coming and why she didn't warn me and why she didn't make sure Peter didn't go.

Did you know?

The river is roaring and I am yelling and I can't hear if Mama is saying anything and then I decide I do not even want to hear what she says anyway so I turn and race toward the house. I think maybe she is calling after me but I do not turn around and I do not go back.

The night is awful. There is an empty spot in the bed for Peter and I won't let Ivy lie in his space, even when she complains why can't she have his spot, since he's not around to roll on top of us anymore. Aunt Eleanor took him so fast he left his measuring tape behind, and I tuck it into the chest at the foot of the bed, nestling it under the someday books Mama left for me.

That night it pours harder than I've ever seen and the boulders in the river roll and thunder and the rain pounds against our roof and then it comes leaking through our ceiling and drips on our bed. I think even the heavens are crying out for Peter.

Anna May and Belle are getting quite worried about me. They want to know why I am thin as a rail. Because of all these chores, I tell them, throwing another string bean in the pot.

Mirabel thinks when you lose your mama and your papa and now your two brothers, the thing is to keep busy. Snapping beans is the best cure, she keeps telling me, for when you are feeling down in the dumps.

I tell her to stop talking like that. I run out and bury my face in Anna May's neck. After a while, there is Mirabel right beside me, handing me another basket of beans.

I am down by the barn giving Minnie and Olympia and Bea the what-for because they have hidden their eggs again where I can't find them.

I hear crying, and first I think it is Birdie, out by the road again. It is not. It is Phoebe. She is ripping her little braids apart, and throwing the little strings on top of the sunflowers that are just poking up. Then she stomps all over everything. She is making quite a mess. Then she sinks down and buries her face in her arms, and I can see her shaking all the way over where I am.

I hear my heart saying I better go over, and of course Anna May and Belle are right there telling me to hurry, Mirabel won't even know.

"Phoebe?"

She looks up at me, soon as I get across the road. Her face is wet.

"Phoebe. What's wrong?"

She puts her face on her lap again. I bend down closer. I think how with that many tears, the sunflowers won't need watering.

"Phoebe?"

"What?"

"What's wrong?" I look over at Anna May and Belle. They have come all the way down to the fence and are telling me to keep trying.

"Phoebe?" I say softly.

"My mama did my hair the right way and Rosalyn does it all stupid," Phoebe says, crying so hard she has to stop talking. Finally, she says, "I don't want Rosalyn anymore. I want my mama."

I look up, and Anna May and Belle are remembering what it feels like to lose someone you love.

I reach over and touch Phoebe's hair, her every-which-way braids all undone. "Oh, Phoebe," I say. "Rosalyn loves you, I know she does."

"Rosalyn is terrible with hair."

"I bet she's better than Mirabel."

Phoebe shakes herself away from me.

"I will do it," I say, finally.

Phoebe cries even more. I'm not expecting this.

"What do you know about my kind of hair, Charlie Anne?"

I look back at Anna May and Belle. "Nothing," I say. "Except I think it's pretty. And you can teach me how."

I keep wondering the next few days if Mirabel will ever see the hole in my heart. She says that after I milk Anna May, I can have some time to myself. She hands me *The Charm of Fine Manners*.

"Keep it in your pocket, and keep looking at it whenever you think to," she says, wiping the biscuit flour off her hands. "Your reading will get better before you know it and you'll be bettering yourself at the same time."

Mirabel picks up a tray of biscuits and puts them in the oven.

"What about Ivy?" I say, looking at the book. "How come she never has to?"

Mirabel shuts the oven door and turns around. "She's started being friends with that Ellis girl, that's why. She's developing plenty of manners over there, I'm quite sure."

"With Miss High-and-Mighty? How can Becky Ellis be better than Phoebe?"

"It is quite clear, Charlie Anne, that you need that

book more than anyone. Why must you make a to-do about absolutely everything? Now go, before I find more work for you."

Anna May doesn't stand still for milking any better than she used to, but at least with Belle close she's happier.

I still have to be very stern with her, though, because Anna May is that kind of cow. I give her my most terrible mad look, just to get things started on the right foot, and then I tell her I am in no mood for any horsing around.

Then I turn soft as butter while I brush her with her favorite cow brush and scratch her behind her ears, and I whisper sweet things in her ears, like what a lovely girl she is and how all the other cows in the world can only wish they were as wonderful as her.

This makes her happy.

Then I scratch her some more and give her some corn, and while she's eating, I set the milk stool on her right side (cows like things to be the same way all the time) and I wash her udder. I tell her in my sweetest voice to behave.

While I am milking, Belle is wondering what the dickens is going on, and I tell her to hold her bonnet, that if Anna May does her job, we will all be out under the butternut tree very quick.

Anna May shifts her weight around and I pull my feet away, because getting stepped on by a cow can make your heart stop beating, it hurts so much. She moos to make sure I am doing everything right. "Yes," I tell her. "I know how to milk a cow."

"How on earth did you get so much?" Mirabel wants to know when I bring the pail up to the house.

"She's happier with Belle here. Cows are happy when you don't take away someone they love."

Mirabel just stares at me. "You are a funny girl," she says slowly. Then she goes back to frying potatoes.

After breakfast I sit on the porch and open *The Charm of Fine Manners*, but the letters get all switched up and I can't make sense of much of it.

Then I hear Phoebe and Rosalyn down by the road, tending to their flowers, and pretty soon my feet are telling me that if I hurry, I can go over for a visit, and Mirabel won't even know.

I rush off, hiding the book in the apple barrel in the barn, and before I can say milk cow, I am jumping over the stone wall and running across the road.

They are replanting the sunflowers that Phoebe mussed up, trying to make the little broken ones stand up again. Phoebe has new ribbons in her hair, and the braids I made for her are looking fine.

"Charlie Anne," says Rosalyn, "we were just talking about you. We are just finishing up. We have a surprise for you inside. Want to come see?"

I nod and I let Rosalyn pull me into the house, where there is a bright yellow dress on the kitchen table that someone has cut up to make over.

"It's for you, Charlie Anne," Phoebe says. "We are making trousers so you can have some, too."

Rosalyn puts wood in the cookstove to heat up her kettle. "Want tea?"

I nod. As long as it's sweet raspberry. I walk over and touch the cloth. It is soft like the fluff on a new chick.

"We thought your dress was a little small, and that maybe you were ready for something that fit you a little better?"

"Well, yes," I say, looking down at my chore dress, and at how it hardly covers up my underpants anymore.

"Have you ever had trousers like this?" Rosalyn wants to know.

I shake my head. "I've never known any girls who wear trousers except for overalls, not until you two."

"I see," says Rosalyn, picking up a pair of scissors and beginning to cut. "Well, *I* think girls should wear trousers if they want to. Do you know why?"

She is looking at me, waiting for an answer.

"Why?"

She looks glad I asked. "Because we do not need to be defined by our circumstances. We can make things different, we can change things, even climb right up and out of the boxes that some people want to put us in. But we have to work hard and we have to decide that we're no quitters and that we're going to succeed at what we set out to do—no matter what. Are you a quitter, Charlie Anne?"

I watch the two of them, Phoebe cutting around the pattern in careful lines and Rosalyn sitting there in red pepper red trousers. I think about Mirabel and what she would say about all this. I shrug because I really don't know if I'm a quitter or not. Maybe I'll talk to Anna May and Belle about it when I get home.

Rosalyn smiles at me. "You let me know what you decide, okay?" Then we cut out the pieces and pin everything together, and I prick myself over and over because sewing is one chore that I cannot do. Then Rosalyn takes the pieces and puts them in her sewing machine, and she pumps the foot pedal up and down, up and down, and before I know it, my trousers are getting sewed. Phoebe asks me if I want to help her make carrot sandwiches, and I say I have never had carrot sandwiches before but I will be pleased to try some and, yes, I will help.

This is how you make them: Peel and then chop up uncooked carrots as fine as you can get them. Put the carrots in a bowl and add a handful of chopped-up salted peanuts (or raisins if you are up north, where no one has any peanuts anyway) and a spoonful of mayonnaise. Spread on warm bread.

Carrot sandwiches go especially nice with a bowl of applesauce and about a hundred cups of sweet raspberry tea.

*   *   *

I eat so much—two sandwiches, two bowls of apple-sauce and all the sweet raspberry tea I can hold—that we are not sure if I will fit in my new yellow trousers, but when they finally come off the sewing machine, they are fitting just fine.

Phoebe and Rosalyn make me stand in the middle of the room with my trousers on because it is pinning time, and they put a bunch of pins in their mouths, and both of them fold and pin where the hems should be. Then I have to take the trousers off and Rosalyn clears all the crumbs off the table and we go over and she gives me a needle and takes one for herself.

While I am learning to hem, Rosalyn asks Phoebe if she will read to us again, and before I know it I am feeling so bad for little David Copperfield and his awful life that tears start welling up in my eyes and then dripping down my face and then Phoebe puts down the book and asks what is the matter and I tell them all about how my life is not turning out so good.

Then Rosalyn reaches over and hugs me and then Phoebe does, too. I am not used to so much hugging since Mama left us, certainly not from a colored girl, not ever, but I pretend that I am used to being hugged a lot. When the hems are done, I put the trousers back on and go look at myself in their mirror and say, Hey, wait a minute, when did you get so tall, anyway?

When I leave a little later, I think that even the sun is not as bright as I am in my new yellow trousers.

I run across the road and into the barn, where I hurry out of my trousers and fold them as small as I can make them and hide them inside the apple barrel and walk back outside as calm as can be so no one can see how happy my heart is feeling about everything. It is a nice change.

"Oh, Charlie *Aaaa-aaaanne!*" I hear from up in the tree by the barn. "We saw you. We saw you over at that house with that colored girl!"

Ivy and Becky Ellis are high in the apple tree, looking down at me. They throw apples on my head.

"We're going to tellllllll on you." Ivy is laughing. "And what's that you were wearing when you went in the barn? Tell us. Was it something yellooow?"

A few more apples fall on my head. "Mirabel told you to stay away from that colored girl, and now you're going to really get the what-for," says Ivy.

Five apples fall on me all at once. Then Ivy starts climbing down.

"Fine, go ahead, Ivy," I say, stepping out of the way of any more falling apples. "At least I'm not spending my time kissing Becky Ellis's shoes."

When I get up to the house, Mirabel tells me to get the clothes on the line. "Take Birdie with you. She's been pestering me all day. Where've you been, anyway?"

Birdie does not understand how when you are with Mirabel, you should not be asking her a hundred questions every five minutes, and you should especially not be asking, "Where is Charlie Anne?"

Just as we are folding the last blanket, Ivy tears past me with a streak of yellow flying behind. Becky is running after her, laughing so hard and staggering so much she looks like she is going to pee.

My heart flips and I let the blanket fall on the ground and I run after Ivy, trying to catch her before she gets any farther with my yellow trousers, which now look like a kite flapping behind her.

Birdie cries, "Stop, Charlie Anne, wait for me, wait for meeeeece." She falls and wails, but I don't stop. Ivy is not the fastest runner in the world. I am gaining on her, and she looks back and shrieks for Mirabel.

I reach Becky first and grab on to the back of her dress and pull and it tears and then Becky falls and screams that her dress is all ruined. Just a few more strides and I will be close enough to overtake Ivy and I pump my arms and look for strength from I know not where and gain on Ivy. But what I am not counting on is that Mirabel will be sitting on the porch, mending.

"What is it with you two?" she says.

"Look!" screams Ivy. "Look what Charlie Anne is hiding." Then Ivy runs right up on the porch and drops my yellow trousers onto Mirabel's lap and Becky is still screaming on the lawn and I know my goose is cooked.

Well. We have to walk Becky home and I have to go, too, because Mirabel is going to make me tell Mrs. Ellis how I ripped Becky's dress and how I am sorry, and I must beg her pardon and use my best manners while I am doing it. We will talk about the trousers and about being with that colored girl when we get home, Mirabel tells me, and this gets Ivy and even Becky laughing, and I tell Becky if she does not quit it, I am going to make sure that more than just her dress is ripped up.

"Are you threatening me, Charlie Anne?" she says in that whiney voice of hers, and I lunge at her, but Mirabel pulls us apart before I can get at her face.

"What's gotten into you?" Mirabel takes Becky's hand and heads toward the Ellis house, and I have to pick up the back of the line, behind Ivy and Birdie, who keeps asking me, "What was that yellow thing, anyway?" and I have to keep saying, "Shush your mouth up, Birdie."

"And don't drag your feet," Mirabel yells back.

Belle and Anna May are watching our parade, and

Belle wants to know why I am looking so miserable. Poor, poor, pitiful Charlie Anne, I tell myself as we walk up the hill, and even Olympia and Minnie and Bea come running out to see where we are all going.

Across the road, Old Mr. Jolly's house is looking all happy with its new door, and now there are sky blue shutters. After a while, I get a little tired of hearing me telling myself what a terrible, troubled life I am having, how nothing is turning out the way I want, and I decide I need to give myself a good talking to, and I do. When I am done, I am feeling all yelled at, and right then and there, as we turn into the Ellis driveway, I tell myself that someday I am going to teach that Ellis family a few manners. Lord knows they need some.

Mrs. Ellis takes one look at Becky all ripped up and dirty and starts boo-hooing, and then she asks about a hundred times, Are you all right, dear? and then she decides Becky is all right, but she gives Mirabel a what-kind-of-family-are-you look anyway.

Mirabel is very unhappy to be standing there, and I bet she is wishing she sent us on our own. Then Mrs. Ellis looks down to see if we have shoes on or not, which of course we do not, and this makes Mirabel's frown come back.

"What shall be done?" Mrs. Ellis wants to know.

Mirabel clears her throat and gives me the

why-aren't-you-apologizing look, and I give Ivy and then Becky my most terrible mad look, and then I turn to Mrs. Ellis and say as mannerly as I can, "Please pardon my bad manners, ma'am."

Ivy and Becky snicker, and I look off back toward Old Mr. Jolly's house and wish more than anything that I were sitting at the table listening to Phoebe reading, and drinking sweet raspberry tea. Instead, I hear Mirabel suggest that maybe I could mend Becky's dress.

Mrs. Ellis thinks about it for a moment and decides it is a good idea. She tells Becky to change and bring back the dress, and while she is at it, to bring the pile of mending from the back parlor that needs doing.

"I am not good at mending," I say.

Mrs. Ellis looks at me sharply. "Children need to learn their place, wouldn't you agree, Mirabel?"

"Well, yes, I certainly do," says Mirabel, and then Becky is standing in front of us with a pile of clothes so high you cannot even see her face, and then Mirabel isn't looking so sure about things.

"If she wasn't Sylvie's child, I wouldn't be so forgiving, you know," Mrs. Ellis says. "Bless that woman's sweet soul, she always had something kind to say to everyone." Then Mrs. Ellis takes the stack of clothes from Becky and piles it into my arms.

"We'll need these back before church on Sunday.

Now off you go, you have a lot of work to do," she says, waving her arm and sending us on our way, without ever once inviting us in.

I am so weighed down under my bundle that I can hardly see Ivy laughing at me the whole way home.

Mirabel puts my trousers in her rag box and tells me to stay away from them, and she decides the only thing to be done is to step up my lessons. Each night she sits in the rocking chair and I sit in the rail-back chair so I can learn to sit up straight without slumping, plus I am learning to mend.

"Tiny stitches," says Mirabel, over and over. She is making us each a new pair of underpants out of feed sacks. My pair has a rooster on the back.

"I'm not wearing those!"

"You will, and you will be grateful to have undergarments. Some girls don't have any at all."

I roll my eyes.

"You don't want to be able to see the stitches, see?" She holds up my new underpants and shows me the seam. She keeps checking to make sure I am sewing in a straight line.

While I am doing this, Mirabel reads:

> We must persistently strive
> against selfishness, ill-temper,

irritability, indolence. It is
impossible for the self-centered or
ill-tempered girl to win love and
friends.

✺

Mirabel looks up at me. "All right, Charlie Anne. Let's think for a moment about what that means." She puts the book on her lap and sits back in her rocking chair and waits for the words to sink into me.

I watch the last of the sun dip down below our barn. I do not know why Ivy does not get these lessons, when she needs them more than me.

"Well?" Mirabel looks over her glasses and straight into me. "What does that mean?"

I take a giant breath and swallow all the words inside of me. I shrug.

"It means that you need a loving, generous nature if you are to get on in this world. I'm surprised you can't see that." And with that, Mirabel is off again:

One of the greatest blemishes
in the character of any young
person, especially of any young
girl or woman, is forwardness,
boldness, pertness. The young girl
who acts in such a manner as to
attract attention in public; who

speaks loudly, and jokes and
laughs and tells stories in order
to be heard by others than her
immediate companions; . . . who
expresses opinions on all subjects
with forward self-confidence, is
rightly regarded by all thoughtful
and cultivated people as one
of the most disagreeable and
obnoxious characters to be met
with in society.

I feel the walls of my heart tightening, boxing me into
this room with Mirabel.

"A quiet and generous spirit. That is what you
should be striving for, Charlie Anne."

27

Oh, happy day! New shoes arrive for all of us from Papa, plus a letter with money and four lemon drops inside. His handwriting is small and pushed together, and I can only read a few words anyway, so Ivy has to read it.

Papa says that thanks to President Roosevelt, the government has a lot of roads it wants built, so there is plenty of work. Thomas is even taller now than Papa. There are new shoes for Peter, so Papa does not know about Aunt Eleanor. He wants Peter to write to him and tell him how high the corn is, and if he is measuring week by week.

I feel my heart splitting for Peter. There is a return address for Papa, and I stuff the envelope in my pocket.

I will try and write to Papa about all that happened to Peter, but first I try on my new shoes. I am so happy to be slipping them on and tying them up and walking around in them that I don't hardly even feel the leather pressing hard on my skin. I tell them if they don't stop snapping when I walk, I'm going to sound just like Mirabel.

I hear Mama calling out to me, telling me to come up and let her have a look at my new shoes, but I tell her no. She should have thought of wanting to see things like new shoes before she let Peter go. Now I have Rosalyn and Phoebe to show things to.

Papa's letter puts Mirabel in a good mood. She tells me I can have the day to myself, "after you finish up that mending."

I make tiny stitches like she tells me. I just don't make a lot of them.

I have to wait about a hundred years to show Phoebe my new shoes. Mirabel has to walk down to the garden and see about the tomatoes and pick some cucumbers and stop at the privy so she can read the Sears catalog for a while. Then she goes and looks at the weeds we call lamb's-quarters, because you can eat them, and she's been thinking of canning them, just in case the hard times are even worse than we're expecting. Then she beats the rug from the parlor against the porch, and next she goes hunting for the place where Minnie is hiding her eggs.

I head out to the butternut tree and tell Anna May and Belle the good news, that Papa is alive and well, and while I do that, I do a little looking for Big Pumpkin Face. I have not seen her in a few days now.

While I am looking inside the barn and the cellar and the hen roosts, I tell her she better be quick and olly olly oxen free and come out. But Big Pumpkin Face stays hidden, and my feet start telling me if I crawl on my belly through the high rye grass and jump quick over the stone wall that Mirabel won't even see. I tell Anna May and Belle to be quiet, and they look at me and wonder what the dickens I am slithering around like an old garden snake for. They come over for a closer look.

"Go away," I say, sounding very stern.

I have a big dirt stain across the back of my dress and a grass stain across my belly, plus there are rips from the blackberry bushes. I run across the road, remembering how I haven't had a bath for several days.

Then Phoebe comes shooting out of the barn on her swing, one arm draped out beside her, and she's wearing her red pepper red trousers, looking graceful as a swan. As she flies back to the barn and then back out again, she points her toes up, and I believe she is tiptoeing and that she could dance straight up to the moon if she wanted. I can hardly breathe.

"A turn," I croak as she soars out past me again. "Please, can I please have a turn?"

"Watch how I do it!" Phoebe screams, laughing, and I have to watch her fly past me over and over again, probably a hundred more times, and she's all particular about the way she points her toes.

"I KNOW HOW TO DO IT, PHOEBE," I say, feeling another frown spread across my face. "I KNOW HOW TO SWING."

Old Mr. Jolly comes walking up from the brier patch, carrying big clippers in his hands. He is watching Phoebe fly right over him. He has cuts on his arm, and his face is looking how my heart is feeling: annoyed, and like maybe Phoebe shouldn't always get to be the luckiest frog in the pond.

"Phoebe," he calls. "I believe your friend here would like a turn."

It takes about a hundred more minutes for Miss Red Pepper Pants to slow down. I am afraid she might see the rooster on my underpants because my dress is so short and Mirabel won't let me near my trousers in the rag box. I think I hear Mama calling me from up on the hill, telling me not to worry about my underpants. I tell her I am still not talking to her. She tells me that she understands and that she is sorry about everything.

I watch to make sure Anna May and Belle are watching me and they are. They are looking up and asking what the dickens I am doing climbing the ladder to the hayloft. I tell them not to worry. I wonder if Phoebe can see my new shoes. I tap a soft little shuffle, I am so happy. Then she soars into the barn and lands on her landing platform and hands the rope up to me.

"Do you remember how to do it?"

"Yes, Phoebe," I say, rolling my eyes. "I know how to swing." Then I jump onto the seat, and I am whooping because suddenly I am more than just Charlie Anne. I am Charlie Anne who can fly.

Rosalyn comes out and tells us that she has some raspberry heart sugar cookies for us.

"Where's your yellow trousers?" she asks as soon as we get up on the porch.

"Mirabel won't let me wear them," I say between one bite and the next. "She says they are for boys."

I see Rosalyn get that shadow over her face again. "Is that so?" she says, munching her cookie. Then she stands up, goes into her parlor, and comes back with a book from the bookshelf. She hands me another cookie. "I brought this book from Mississippi. I thought we might try a page or two."

My breathing stops. Just the cover, with the words *First Reader* on it, sends my memory flying back to how it used to be with Miss Moran and the terrible place under her desk she made me go when I switched up my words.

"*Saw* is not the same thing as *was*. I don't see why you keep mixing things up," she'd say. There were spiders and dead flies under there and Becky Ellis would laugh.

"No," I say to Rosalyn, standing up. "I don't like that book very much."

Both she and Phoebe are looking confused. "Thank you for the cookies," I mumble, and I hurry out, because even mending is better than that book.

I go look some more for Big Pumpkin Face. I look everywhere. All around the grain bins and the apple barrels and the chicken coop, up in the loft (three times) and down by the pigpen. I call to her over and over and over.

I stop and give Minnie and Olympia and Bea a good lookover to make sure they don't know where she is hiding. Olympia wants a handful of corn, but I tell her she's not getting any on account of her being such a tight-fisted old hen. That's what Papa used to say.

I am thinking about Papa when Big Pumpkin Face meows from the hayloft. "What are you doing up there?" I say, hurrying up the ladder and not paying a bit of attention to Olympia, who is making mad looks at my back.

"Here, kitty. Here, kitty," I say to the dark corners, and then very big purrs come out from deep inside a stack of hay. I kneel down and look into the dark tunnel between bales, and smell a lot of hay all at once. It is the best smell in the world, just like dried-out sunshine. I sniff lots of times as I'm trying to get my eyes to see better in the dark.

I lift the bales out of the way, and when I do, one of

them is singing happy news. I pull the next hay bale with soft hands, and the next ones I just push a little out of the way. And there she is! Right in front of me is my Big Pumpkin Face, looking all proud, because nestled up to her are three new kittens.

I scream a very big whoop. "Why didn't you tell me you were going to be a mama? I would have made you a nice basket." I sit back on my heels and watch. "I thought you were eating too much, you big bugbear." I scratch her a little behind her ear, but she pushes closer to her babies, so I stop. I reach over and rub a little black kitten, but Big Pumpkin Face mews that I better knock it off right now, so I stop and sit back on my heels. I don't try and pick up the kittens, even though I want to more than just about anything.

Big Pumpkin Face is singing happy mews to them and I don't want her to stop, so I just watch them and remember how I used to like to climb up on my mama's bed, right between her and Papa, when I had the middle-night scares. Every so often, Big Pumpkin Face licks one of the babies. I think she looks happy to be a mama. My mama used to look as happy as Big Pumpkin Face.

The sun is shining through the window of the barn and splashing all over me and the happy new family, and as I sit on my heels and watch them, I hear Mirabel calling me and yelling that they are going to walk to

Evangeline's and where am I, and I think, who wants to go to the store when you can stay and watch new kittens. The sun warms my skin. It has been a long hard summer without Papa. I curl up on the hay, watching the mama cat and her kittens. I feel myself falling asleep, and I hear Mama telling me that everything always looks better after a nap.

29

You can tell Rosalyn is worried she did something wrong, because I wake up to Phoebe calling for me and carrying a big basket of something that smells so warm and buttery that Big Pumpkin Face and I can smell it way up in the loft.

"What's in there?" I want to know.

"It's for you. Can I come up?"

Well. Phoebe is bringing two tiny pies, each with a crust that smells like butter, and each has a mountain of glistening strawberries on top. I take a bite and can't believe how happy my tongue is. Rosalyn knows how to cook. She has the same things as Mirabel, but she turns a pile of strawberries into strawberry tarts and Mirabel makes strawberry fool.

Phoebe sees the kittens and gives a little happy yelp.

"Big Pumpkin Face, this is Phoebe. Phoebe, this is Big Pumpkin Face and all her new kittens."

Phoebe says lots of things like Oh, my! and How cute! and You are so lucky, Charlie Anne, and then she picks up the little orange one that looks just like Big Pumpkin Face and rubs it behind the ears. I am surprised Big Pumpkin Face lets her, but she does.

We sit admiring the kittens and I eat both strawberry tarts and my belly is sticking out.

"Rosalyn wants to know how come you got so upset and how come you don't want to read that book?"

I pack the little tart plates back in the basket and wipe my hands on the bottom of my dress. I tell the bad thoughts to go away, that I don't want to be thinking about them right now, that I don't want to remember the underneath of Miss Moran's desk, or the even worse places.

"The words jumble up when I read."

"Like what?"

"Like *bed* and *dad*. It looks like the same thing."

"Yes," says Phoebe, "they are close," and while she says this, I am thinking about Miss Moran.

"How come you don't know the words *they*, *what*, *where*, *does*?" Miss Moran is saying. I am standing for my reading drill and everyone is watching. Mama has already gone straight to heaven and I am very lonely. I look out the window.

"Stand up straight, Charlotte Anne," Miss Moran is saying. "Self-composure and self-confidence are most important. Straighten that back. All right, now read."

I look at the book I am holding, *First Reader*, where the letters are jumping like corn popping. Miss Moran sighs, again and again and again.

"I am losing patience with your lack of attention, Charlotte Anne."

I squint my eyes and stumble on the words. Miss Moran stops me. "How come you don't know this when we practice every day? Are you just fooling with me, Charlotte Anne?"

"No, ma'am, I am not." I see the blackboard giving me comforting looks.

"Well, I think you are fooling me," Miss Moran says, walking closer. "I think you are trying to make a joke of my class to get a little attention. Otherwise, why would your sister be so much better at reading than you? She's not that much older. Now you just go stand in that trash bucket over there until you remember what we've been practicing every day for the last week."

Even Ivy is looking all sorry for me as I walk over and step into the trash bucket. But no one is sorry as me when we have our spelling bees.

"Spell *bad*. We do not like bad little girls."

I have no stomach anymore. It has already fallen all the way down to my feet. I am hot, and sweat is pouring down my face, and sweat is making my back itch, but I'm afraid to scratch it because Miss Moran will get mad. I can't remember how to spell *bad*. I can't remember if it has *d*s or *b*s. I can't remember what the first letter is, and I can't remember what the last letter is, and I can't remember what is in the middle.

*b*s and *d*s look the same to me. I think they do a

little dance, and one day they are one way and another day they are a different way. I tell them to stop fooling with me, but the bs and ds, they just don't listen.

Miss Moran is already plenty mad. "Spell *bad*, Charlotte Anne."

I take a gulp of air. Thomas is looking all sad for me. Even then, his legs were so long he couldn't keep them under the desk.

I take a deep breath and feel tears coming. *"D-a-d."*

Miss Moran throws her cleaning rag at me. All she has to do is point outside. I already know what she means.

I pick up my lunch pail and go outside to the woodshed so I can think about things. I sit on a pile of oak logs the rest of the day, and while I am there, it starts to snow.

"Was it really like that?" Phoebe wants to know. "Was it really that bad?"

"Yes, it was."

We look at Big Pumpkin Face and are quiet.

Then Phoebe sits back on her heels. "You have to sweep out all the bad memories inside of you and start over again," she says. "That's what Rosalyn says."

"Bosh."

"Bosh?"

"Bosh."

I scratch Big Pumpkin Face right behind the ears, just like she likes. She starts purring.

"I have lots of bad memories, too," whispers Phoebe.

"My mama was tall, taller even than Rosalyn," Phoebe says as we both watch Big Pumpkin Face get up for a minute and stretch and then lie right back down next to her kittens.

"That is why you are tall," I say.

"Yes," says Phoebe, settling back against a bale of hay. "Now stop interrupting. It's a long story, and I don't like to stop when I get going."

"Okay." I settle back against a hay bale, too. My stomach is very uncomfortable from being so full of strawberry tarts. I lie down on my side.

"Well, my mama and Rosalyn lived together when they were little and they were best friends, and when they grew up, they wanted to go to college together, but my mama couldn't go to Rosalyn's school because she was colored."

Phoebe reaches over and pats one of the kittens and Big Pumpkin Face lets her.

"So my mama worked hard and saved her money and went to a different school, one for colored girls who wanted to be teachers.

"She and Rosalyn stayed friends and wrote to each

other and planned how one day they would open a school where everyone could sit side by side, no matter what color your skin was."

The sun is getting really warm, and it is beating through the window and making me a little sleepy again. Plus Phoebe's voice is so gentle and soft, like breathing. I have to force my eyes to stay open.

"When Rosalyn finished school and came back home, my mama already had me by this time, and during the years when I was little, they planned the school they would open someday. And then they did, right in an old school way out in the woods that no one used anymore, and Rosalyn took out a notice in the paper announcing the school and that all were welcome, and on the day we started, no white children came."

"None?"

"Not a one."

"What dopes."

"Yes," whispered Phoebe. "A whole bunch of little colored children came, but not a single white one. And then things started happening."

I am wide awake again. "Like what?"

"Like someone threw a dead chicken in the schoolyard one day when I was helping Mama wash windows. And someone started nailing notes on the door telling us to move out of town, that no white child would ever get taught by a colored teacher. They called Rosalyn all

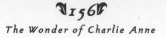

kinds of dirty bad names for being friends with my mama."

Tears start down Phoebe's face. I pull her close and tell her she doesn't have to tell me any more if she doesn't want to. We can still be friends without telling each other all the bad places that need sweeping out.

I feel her collarbone poking into me. Her little braids are digging into my neck.

"We found out some of the men who owned stores in town started threatening the colored mamas and papas and telling them that if they sent their children to that school, we would all see it go up in flames.

"Mama got really mad because her grandmother had been born a slave in Kentucky and had seen it all. She said we weren't going back to any of that, no way, no how. She would rather die first." She wipes her eyes, and keeps going.

"My mama and Rosalyn were like sisters, they loved each other so. One day we all walked to the library in our city, but my mama and I couldn't go to the shelves where Rosalyn went because they wouldn't let us read the books set aside for white people. Rosalyn checked out the books, and we read them together outside under a big sycamore tree."

"What books?"

Phoebe smiles for a tiny bit. "One was *David Copperfield*."

"Good book," I say.

"Yes. Well, anyway, there were water fountains in town, one for whites to drink and one for colored people. When no one was looking, I drank from the one for whites."

"Did it taste different?"

"No, you silly. Water is water."

Phoebe stops to scratch Big Pumpkin Face some more.

"We kept opening the school every day, and I had the job of ringing the bell, but I was ringing it to no one but the trees. Then we'd shut the door, and Mama and Rosalyn would read to me and I would read to them. That's how I got to be such a good reader. They paid all their attention to me.

"One day, when we were walking home, a big cart comes flying up the road, and a man is yelling for Mama to get out of the way of his horses, that no one wants her teaching in this town, but she doesn't get out of the way, she doesn't budge, and Rosalyn pushes me out of the way just in time, and that was the last time I saw my mama alive."

Phoebe starts shaking and I hold her and she cries for a long time and my head is hurting from the whole painful story.

"Now that we've told each other our sad stories, we're best-friend sisters," I tell Phoebe as we start putting the hay bales back to hide Big Pumpkin Face.

"I know another way," Phoebe says, standing up. "We can be real blood sisters. We just have to prick our fingers."

I give her my what-are-you-talking-about look. I have never heard of such a thing.

"My mama and Rosalyn did it when they were our age. Come here, I'll show you." She walks over to the window so she can see better. She pulls a pin off the waistband around her trousers. "Here, like this."

I watch as Phoebe gives her finger a tiny prick and see a little drop of blood coming up.

"Now you do it."

She hands the pin to me.

The thought of being sisters with Phoebe is pretty nice, especially when I have a sister as bad as Ivy. But I'm not so sure about pricking myself.

"Come on, it doesn't hurt." She holds the pin closer.

I look at it. I look at the drop of blood sitting on her finger and I think about how much pricking yourself hurts. I feel myself getting woozy and take a step back.

Phoebe is starting to laugh. "Are you mousey?" She pushes the pin closer to my finger.

"What does that mean, are you mousey?"

"What, you don't say that up here?"

"No, we don't. We are nice to people who are about to bleed to death."

Phoebe is laughing now. "Mousey means scaredy-cat," she says.

"Oh," I say, and I look at the pin and how it is coming closer to my finger and I think about the blood sitting on her finger and how pretty soon there will be blood sitting on my finger and how everything is getting all dark and I start falling backward and I can't tell if she's pricking my finger or not.

When I wake up, Phoebe is looking all worried, then she hits me. "What are you doing, scaring me like that?"

I am feeling very confused. "Why are you hitting me?"

"You fainted!" Then Phoebe starts laughing again. "I never saw anyone faint before over a drop of blood. You sure are mousey."

"I am not," I say, standing up and giving her my most terrible mad look, the one I give only to Anna May when she kicks over the milk bucket, and to Papa when he is about to leave for a long, long time.

"I am not mousey. And I don't like to be laughed at. That's rule number one, if we're going to be best-friend sisters." I am glaring at her. She stops laughing.

"Blood sisters," she says, holding up her finger. "We're blood sisters."

* * *

Phoebe goes home after that and I go down by Anna May and Belle and suck on my finger and while I am down there Mama is whispering how she told me things would be better after my nap, now didn't she.

3

Phoebe starts lighting a candle in her window every night. I light one right back to say yes, yes, I will meet you tomorrow as soon as I can get away from Mirabel, and I blow it out quick because I hear Ivy coming up the stairs.

Mirabel doesn't have time to check up on me much because after the ragman came with his wagon filled with hand-me-downs, screaming, "Rags! Rags!" she is getting clothes ready for us for the winter. She is knitting hats and mittens and socks after unwinding someone's old sweaters and she's making over a new dress for each of us. This means she pulls apart some old lady's dress and cuts it smaller and sews the whole thing up again.

I like trousers better, I tell her when she makes me try on a dress, and she is so mad she spits the pins in her mouth out on the floor.

She makes Ivy sit right beside her and take out all the seams and hem everything, and Birdie is clipping the threads. "You two are really good at sewing," she tells them. I give Ivy my smirking look. She throws the pincushion at me.

"They're better homemakers," Mirabel tells me,

shooing me to take out the compost and milk Anna
May and collect the eggs.

Thank God, I think.

"Just be sure to stay away from that colored girl."

I keep my secret to myself, that we are already blood
sisters, and nothing can keep us apart.

Nothing? asks Belle when I get down by the butternut tree.

Nothing, says Anna May.

"You've got that right." I kiss Belle and Anna May
on the nose. "Nothing can keep blood sisters apart."
They look at me all warmhearted, and then Anna May
licks my cheek with her sandpaper tongue. "How can
Mirabel know so little when you know so much?" I look
into Anna May's eyes and press my face deep into her
neck, smelling her sweet warm cow smell. Belle takes
time to scratch her head slowly on the big rock beside
us. That's the thing about cows. They know when it's
time to relax.

It is only a quick hop and a quick jump over the stone
wall and across the road. I don't have to knock anymore, Rosalyn tells me, so I don't, and when I open the
door, there is Phoebe sitting on the kitchen table with
her feet swinging over the side. Old Mr. Jolly is standing
right beside her, combing out her hair, and Rosalyn is
holding all sorts of creams and lotions and new ribbons

made from the red pepper red cloth. They are fussing over Phoebe the way mamas and papas like to do.

"I taught them how," Phoebe says, holding up a mirror to make sure they don't make any mistakes.

I sit sipping sweet raspberry tea and watching Old Mr. Jolly comb one teeny bit of hair at a time. Mama keeps whispering that she misses me, and I sigh for a minute, just watching Phoebe getting loved like that, and forgetting all my troubles, but then I remember how Peter is gone and I tell Mama to go away.

Old Mr. Jolly tugs too hard and Phoebe cries out and then Old Mr. Jolly asks Rosalyn to sing something tender so he will be gentle with the combing.

Rosalyn, in that soft buttercup voice of hers, starts off:

> *Butterfly wings, butterfly wings, my baby*
> *has butterfly wings.*
> *She is so special, she is so fine, my Phoebe*
> *has butterfly wings.*

Mmmmmm, I think as I watch Rosalyn divide Phoebe's hair and then twist it into braids that aren't quite so every which way as before. In fact, they are better than mine.

When they are done, Phoebe looks in the mirror for a long time. Then she grins and I can tell her heart is doing hallelujahs, over and over again.

32

Rosalyn hasn't given up on our church, even though Mr. and Mrs. Aldrich, Birdie and I are the only ones who ever eat from her sharing plate.

"Some of them might not have the sense that God gave geese, but that doesn't mean they won't get new feathers. God's good that way," Rosalyn says as she finishes up a batch of raspberry heart sugar cookies.

Mirabel tells Ivy she can go and sit in the back balcony of the church with Becky Ellis. Even I know this is a very bad idea. Ivy tells me with her eyes that I better not say anything or I'll be sorry, and I wonder why Mirabel can't see what is right in front of her nose—a disaster waiting to happen.

The door opens and I stop paying attention to Ivy because Rosalyn, Phoebe and Old Mr. Jolly walk in. There is whispering (mostly from Mrs. Ellis), and some warm friendly smiles (mostly from me and Birdie and Mr. and Mrs. Aldrich). Then the preacher comes in and looks down at us over his thick glasses and then he begins another sermon on sinning and this time he is waving his arms quite a bit and saying that only the righteous are going to get seats at the heavenly banquet and I'm pretty sure I don't even want to go, not if Becky and Mrs. Ellis get seats.

I look out the window and wonder where the mockingbird is and if she's heard one sermon too many and knows to stay away on Sunday mornings. Just as the preacher starts winding down, a pumpkin seed hits me on the back of the neck, and when I turn around, Ivy and Becky are trying to keep from falling off the balcony, they are laughing so hard.

The organ starts getting us ready for "Amazing Grace," and I am so happy to be done hearing about the pit for the wicked that I sing really loud to get myself in a better mood and maybe to make Phoebe giggle, and then Mirabel takes my arm and pulls me to her and whispers in my ear that young ladies do not need to be so noisy.

Then it is announcement time. The preacher starts things off by saying the church will be having its annual fall cleanup and that everyone must come and help rake the yard and cover the roses and wash the windows and paint the things that need painting.

Then Becky stands up in the balcony. "Tryouts will begin after church next Sunday for our Christmas play. Anyone who wants a part has to come."

We'll just see about that. We do the same play every year, and every year I tell them how I want to be the angel, but since Becky is the only one who actually owns a pair of gossamer wings, she gets the part. Last year they made me be the donkey.

Becky sits down, and I am glad when Mrs. Aldrich raises her hand next.

"Mrs. Morrell has been sick with the influenza for a week. Perhaps we could take turns helping. I'm afraid those girls will run out of food if we don't do something."

Mrs. Aldrich says Mrs. Thatcher has been sick with the influenza, too, and that maybe we could help them out as well, and I am halfway standing up to say that we should not, we should not be helping those Thatchers, but Mirabel grabs hold of my arm and pulls me back down.

Then Rosalyn stands up. "Perhaps getting the children of some of these families into school would be a good thing to do while the mothers are recuperating."

I am so proud of her. She reminds me of a good fence post, the way she stands up so straight.

"I would like to open your school and apply for the job of teacher. I received my teacher training in Mississippi and have taught children of all ages, from the youngest to the oldest." She looks down at Phoebe and then up to all the faces watching her. "I would consider it an honor to teach your children."

She sits down. Two more pumpkin seeds come flying

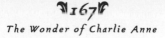

overhead. I'm surprised the preacher doesn't see, but he's taken off his glasses, and I don't think he can see very well even when he has them on.

Rosalyn squeezes Phoebe's shoulder and stands up again. "I shall have Phoebe as my assistant. Her reading ability is extraordinary, which Charlie Anne can attest to." Rosalyn looks over at me and winks, and I feel Mirabel's eyes pinning me to my seat. "Phoebe will assist me with the younger children so I can give more attention to the older students," Rosalyn says, and sits back down.

Mrs. Ellis gasps. Another pumpkin seed comes flying and lands on the floor in front of me. I scoop it up and wait until I have a chance to pelt it back. There is a bunch more whispering, then another pumpkin seed comes flying.

Finally, Mrs. Ellis raises her hand. "The Ladies' Club was going to announce plans to look for a teacher in Boston."

No one says anything. Then Old Mr. Jolly stands up. "We don't need a teacher from Boston. We *have* a teacher right here." He is getting red about the ears. He holds on to Rosalyn's shoulder.

The whispers start flying around the back of the church. I hear Zella behind me. "A colored girl, teaching? Not in my town."

"To think she even suggested it," says Mrs. Reilly.

Old Mr. Jolly squeezes Rosalyn's shoulder and he sits down. My face is burning. I am holding the pumpkin seed so tightly my fingers are numb. Phoebe starts slumping into Rosalyn. I think maybe she is losing her light. No wonder. Who could take all that whispering and still sit up straight?

I hear Mama calling me. I'm not talking to you, I tell her.

Charlie Anne, stand up.

What?

Stand up.

No.

You can't let them hurt your friend.

I'm not standing up.

If you don't do anything, who will?

You, Mama. You could do something, just like you could have done something for Peter.

Mrs. Ellis stands up. "I want to improve my daughter's situation, not make it worse. With all respect, ma'am," she says, nodding to Rosalyn, "we need a teacher from Boston, one who's been properly educated and who can lead us in the right direction."

Rosalyn pops back up. "I know how to teach."

Mrs. Ellis pulls out her fan and starts waving it in front of her face. "You are not the biggest problem, Mrs. Jolly," she says, looking right at Phoebe.

I suck in my breath so fast it shoots down to my toes. The preacher stands up. He is searching for his glasses. "Perhaps we could settle this with a committee," he says, finally.

Old Mr. Jolly stands. "We don't need a committee. We have an educated woman right here willing to do the job."

"Our town is backwater enough," says Mrs. Ellis, snickering behind her fan.

Charlie Anne, stand up.

No.

Charlie Anne, maybe the time for me doing something is over. But maybe the time for you doing something is now.

There is a bunch of whispering behind me. My mouth is so dry. I turn and give Zella and Mrs. Ellis and Becky and Ivy and all the others my most terrible mad look. And then I stand up.

Good girl.

It seems I should say something when I am just standing here, but I do not know what to say. I look at Phoebe and how she is slumping. I take a deep breath.

"You cannot love someone when you do not know someone," I tell everybody. "And you have somebody here you do not know."

Phoebe is looking at me like why am I standing up like this in church, and then I say excuse me to the preacher, because I do know something about manners now, and I hurry over to my friend.

I try and pull Phoebe and she does not budge, so

I stand there and look at everyone. "There's a light inside of her. I thought you might like to know."

Another pumpkin seed comes flying past me and hits Mrs. Aldrich, and she swipes at her neck, thinking she has been bitten by something. There is some muffled laughing from the balcony, and Phoebe is telling me with her eyes to sit down. Rosalyn is looking all surprised at what I am doing, and Old Mr. Jolly is looking like he is wishing he were back clearing out the brier patch.

I clear my throat. Then very softly, in my usual croak, I begin:

Amazing Grace, how sweet the sound,
That saved a soul like me . . .

Most of the people around me are sitting with their mouths hanging straight open. The preacher is turning red.

I sing even louder:

I once was lost but now am found,

Becky has found the old donkey costume in the balcony and is waving it at me. Ivy is bent over, holding her stomach, laughing.

Was blind, but now I see.

Phoebe is just sitting there, looking like a moth trying to escape. It's too late to stop now, I've already gone and started something, and even though I feel Mirabel's iron-hot eyes on me, and the room is full of gasps and astonishment that I am standing up and singing a hymn we've already sung and making a mess of church services, I get the next part out:

> *'Twas Grace that taught my heart to fear,*
> *And Grace my fears relieved.*

And then I realize that Rosalyn's soft-as-buttercups voice is sounding right beside me, and even though Mirabel is frowning a huge frown, Rosalyn makes me feel like I might as well really belt things, and I do:

> *How precious did that Grace appear*
> *The hour I first believed.*

Then—and here's the thing I'm not expecting— Old Mr. Jolly starts joining in, and before he hardly opens his mouth, Mr. and Mrs. Aldrich pop up and they are singing with big grins on their faces.

And then we are done and the church is quiet.

"Well," says Mrs. Ellis.

Rosalyn holds her hand out to Phoebe, and Phoebe takes it and stands up, and Old Mr. Jolly takes her other hand, and together they walk to the door. Phoebe stops and looks at it all shut for a minute, and then she turns around. I see the ironing board down her back again. Then finally, finally, in a voice so soft that only a few of us can hear, she whispers, "Amazing Grace, how sweet the sound."

And then she takes a deep breath and starts over, and she's singing the first verse again, the one about the blind seeing and the lost getting found, and it is like a bell sounding all through our town, and I, for one, am glad to hear it ringing. You can see folks looking amazed, because they never heard an angel sing before.

"Imagine that," I hear Old Mr. Jolly say as he opens the door and walks his new family outside.

Yes, I tell Mama. Imagine that.

33

"You've really done it this time, Charlie Anne," says Ivy, laughing as we all get out of church.

I am looking for Phoebe, but there are so many people crowding on the steps that I can't get through.

"What were you thinking, child?" asks Zella when I finally make it a little way out the door.

"Shame on you, stirring things up like that," says Mrs. Ellis. "You must know it can't come to any good. We can't have a colored girl teaching in this town."

"Why not?"

"Because we'll be even more backwater than we already are. I'm surprised you can't see that, Charlie Anne. Don't you think we're already backwater enough?"

I look back at Mrs. Ellis. She looks like a cross between Olympia and Bea. "Yes," I say slowly, a smile starting. "I think we are."

When I finally find Phoebe and Rosalyn and Old Mr. Jolly, they are standing by the fence talking to Mr. and Mrs. Aldrich about opening the school, and Rosalyn is saying she thinks they should go have a look inside and get things started.

"What are you waiting for?" Mrs. Aldrich says.

"Don't worry about getting paid," says Mr. Aldrich. "We've got a little tucked in an old jar and we've been looking for a good place to put it."

"Backwater or not," says Mrs. Aldrich, "we can pay a good teacher when we find one." Then Mr. Aldrich takes her arm and they walk out onto the road.

"You were really brave," I say, turning to Phoebe.

"You were, too," she says, and then I remember how we are blood sisters and I put my arms around her, and then Mirabel is right beside us, pulling at me, brushing Phoebe's fingerprints off my arm and saying it is time to go home.

Rosalyn notices and steps closer. "I hope you will send the children to school."

"We'll see," says Mirabel, holding on to my arm and trying to steer me to the road. She already has Birdie's hand in a firm grip.

"You know," says Rosalyn, "it is against every law I know of to keep a child out of school who wants to go. Now that the school has a teacher and an assistant willing and able, you might want to send those children to school."

"We'll see," says Mirabel again, really pushing me now.

"Charlie Anne especially wants to go," says Rosalyn,

stepping forward and blocking our path. "I understand she's not reading well, but I've worked with children like her, and all she needs is a little time, a little confidence and a little practice."

Mirabel's frown is growing. "I've been helping Charlie Anne at home. Plus she's learning manners at the same time. Lord knows she needs some."

Then she steers me around Rosalyn and herds us all down the hill. We carry our shoes because our feet are hurting so bad. Even Ivy.

I learn that the cure for standing up for your friend in church is the same as when you are feeling down in the dumps.

"But it is Sunday," I say. "Aren't we supposed to be resting?"

"It is tomato harvest time," says Mirabel. "There is no day like the present to get a chore done."

This is what you do at tomato harvest time. First, you each get a big garden basket, even Ivy, and you rush through the hot grass to the garden, being careful of your blistering feet, because the clover is in full bloom and there are a hundred honeybees to every step you take. Halfway down the hill, you lift Birdie up and carry her, and she puts the baskets on her head to hide from the bees.

Anna May and Belle look up as we go by because

they are wondering why we're not all under the butternut tree, where they are enjoying the afternoon. "Mind your business," I tell them.

When you get to the garden, you pick every last row clean of ripe tomatoes, slapping the gnats away from your neck and ears the whole time. You are very careful of touching a tomato hornworm because they blend into the leaves. When Ivy screeches, and starts jumping up and down and howling, Birdie and I don't even have to ask what she is screaming about. Hornworms are the most revolting things God ever made.

"I quit," says Ivy.

She storms away, but I am yelling after her, "You leave and Mirabel will make you do it all yourself. You know she will, Ivy." Ivy is still walking. The sun is turning Birdie's scalp red. A gnat has gotten inside my ear. "Come to think of it, Ivy, just go!" I scream. "Then you can do all the work yourself."

Ivy stops where she is, and stands there. You can see her start to shake. You can tell she is crying.

She stomps back down to us. "I hate all this work. I hate it so much. Mama never made us do so much work. She took us on picnics. Remember?" The tears are falling terribly fast.

You can tell when Ivy is standing there looking at us, her face stained from all the sorrow, that she was loved once by someone who knew how to love. Just like me.

* * *

Mirabel is waiting back in the kitchen, getting the cookstove hot with who knows how much wood so she can get a huge pot of water boiling. While the sun is steaming and spitting through the windows, we are sweating at the table, washing the tomatoes, and then Mirabel puts them in the hot water. Then back they come, and we have to peel their skins off and cut them into quarters and toss them in a kettle.

Mirabel doesn't want to can plain old tomatoes. That would be too easy. She wants to make stewed tomatoes, which are about one hundred times more work. We end up slicing so many tomatoes that tomato juice is running down our arms and making little tracks in the dirt still on our skin. It stings in all the places the gnats found.

Next, we cut up onions, so our eyes are stinging worse than our arms, and then we chop two dozen peppers, and finally, we add salt and sugar. This all simmers on the cookstove, which means the kitchen is now hotter than a fire pit.

For supper, Mirabel fixes cheese, bread and tall cups of fresh milk from Anna May. We bring it out on the porch, where it is cool.

"Charlie Anne, I want you to listen particularly," Mirabel says as she pulls the manners book from her pocket. As soon as Mirabel starts, Birdie crawls over on my lap.

The young person who would
cultivate tact in speech and
manners will carefully guard
against obtrusiveness.

✂

Mirabel looks over her glasses at us. "Does anyone
know what that means?"

Ivy giggles. "It means don't do what Charlie Anne
did today at church."

I glare at Ivy.

"Yes," says Mirabel. "That's right. We don't need to
stand up in church and get things all riled up."

The next day, Rosalyn and Old Mr. Jolly are loading mops, brooms, rags and buckets into the back of Old Mr. Jolly's truck. I can't help but notice them, and my feet tell me they can't hardly stand still, so don't blame them if they run over without me. I tell them I'm already running.

Old Mr. Jolly is picking up Phoebe and flying her around the driveway before hoisting her into the back of the truck. He isn't so stooped over anymore, I notice. . Phoebe is giggling. "Want to come and help us clean the school?"

Then Old Mr. Jolly comes and asks me if I am going or not. I don't want to go back to that school and see that place under Miss Moran's desk, but I do want him to pick me up so I can laugh as loud as Phoebe, so I let him. I miss my papa very much.

The little white schoolhouse is tucked between two maple trees that are already turning scorched orange. Fall is coming early.

Old Mr. Jolly picks Phoebe and me up and flies us down to the ground, and we screech a little and beg him to do it again. But he says he's getting too old for that sort of thing. I look at him, though—at how his hair isn't hardly gray at all anymore, not since Rosalyn has been cutting all the gray out, and I think he could lift us a hundred times if he wanted to.

Then he hands us mops and brooms and everyone walks to the door, everyone but me.

"What is the matter with you, Charlotte Anne?"

I am remembering Miss Moran pointing to the words she just wrote on the blackboard, pressing her finger against the letters so hard her knuckle is white. "That is a *d* for *dog* and that is a *b* for *ball*."

She tells me to write them on the blackboard, each twenty times. I do. Then she tells me to stand at her desk for my drill. "Hold your book up, keep your back straight, now read that column right there."

She points to my book. I tell my belly to stop doing summersaults because it is making everything worse. All the *d*s and *b*s are switching places, and I cannot tell which is which. "*Ball*."

"No. That is *doll*."

Miss Moran looks out to the class to see if this is a joke, if anyone is laughing, if everyone is in on my joke.

Becky is laughing. So is the oldest Thatcher boy. Sarah Morrell is already crying.

Miss Moran points to the door. "The woodshed. Go to the woodshed until the superintendent gets here."

I am fighting back tears as I pick up my lunch bucket and my coat. The oldest Thatcher boy sticks his foot out into the aisle, but I step around it and go wait in the woodshed for Mr. Pritten and his paddle. It is going to be a long terrible wait.

Everything is the same, just as Miss Moran left it, that's the funny thing. The desks are still lined up in five rows, and her desk is still in the front.

There's a blackboard behind where she sat, and the words she was trying to get me to read are still written in her big printing.

There is a picture of Abraham Lincoln looking at me, and one of George Washington, too, plus a map of New England. The trash bucket is still sitting beside the teacher's desk, and there is a stack of *First Reader* and *Second Reader* and *Third Reader* books.

Old Mr. Jolly comes in with an armload of wood and gets the woodstove started, and Rosalyn puts a box on the teacher's desk and starts pulling out potatoes, butternut squash, onions, garlic, a big pot, plus a loaf of bread, a cup of butter, some coffee, cream, sugar, cups, bowls and spoons.

"We'll make a soup," she says while I am wondering what vegetables are doing in school.

"Learning takes a lot of energy, Charlie Anne. At this school, we'll make a soup every morning and then we'll have something hot for lunch."

Phoebe and I get the job of getting water from the well, which used to be Peter's job, back when Miss Moran was here. When we are back inside, Rosalyn wants us to peel and cut up all the vegetables, then she puts everything into the pot and sets it on the stove, which Old Mr. Jolly has gotten blazing.

We spend the rest of the morning sweeping and mopping and dusting and clearing cobwebs out of the corners and washing the windows. Old Mr. Jolly scrubs the blackboard, and I am happy to see Miss Moran's sentences erased. Then he tells us stories about how he went to school here and how one day a bat flew around the school and the teacher fainted, and I think that if that ever happened to us, Rosalyn wouldn't be afraid. She'd get the bat out. Then Rosalyn tells us her dreams for what kind of school she wants to open: a school for everyone, and then she writes a welcome to the students, and Phoebe has to read it to me because the letters are all jumbled up.

> WHATEVER YOU ARE, BE NOBLE.
> WHATEVER YOU DO, DO WELL.
> WHENEVER YOU SPEAK, SPEAK KINDLY.
> BRING JOY WHEREVER YOU DWELL.

When we are done cleaning, we each have a big bowl of golden harvest soup, and I wonder if Miss Moran ever once thought of filling us up.

*   *   *

"Do you punish the ones who can't read?" It has taken me half the day to get to the question I really need to ask.

"Punish?" says Rosalyn. "What on earth for?" She stops sweeping under the teacher's desk and looks at me.

"Like make them stand in the trash bucket or make them go out to the woodshed or sit under the desk. Stuff like that."

"Is that what the last teacher did?"

I nod my head.

"We will not punish here, Charlie Anne. We won't have time. We'll be too busy growing readers."

I breathe out very slowly and have another helping of soup. As we are leaving, Rosalyn tells Old Mr. Jolly she won't be needing that trash bucket anymore and how maybe he better throw it outside.

Old Mr. Jolly flies Phoebe and me back up on the truck. Phoebe and I stretch out between the mops and brooms and buckets and let the sun shine all over us, and I watch Phoebe close her eyes. Then I hear Mama calling and I tell her I'm not listening, but she keeps calling and calling, and I tell her to stop, but she won't. That's when I see the shadow in the woods, and I hear Mama saying *Watch out, watch out, Charlie Anne!* and I duck as a rock flies out from behind a birch tree, but not soon enough. For just an instant, I see shards of glass inside my head and then about a hundred angry knives against my cheek, and I slump against Phoebe and everything goes black, everything except for the spot between the trees where I saw the oldest Thatcher boy step out.

Phoebe is screaming when I come to and Old Mr. Jolly and Rosalyn are climbing up on the back of the truck and Phoebe is cradling my head in her lap and then they are all trying to stop the bleeding. Old Mr. Jolly jumps off the truck and runs into the woods, but a while later he comes out shaking his head.

Rosalyn holds me as Old Mr. Jolly drives us slowly home. Rosalyn is keeping a cloth pressed against my cheek, and she sighs and tells Phoebe maybe they should forget the whole idea, how maybe opening a school here is too dangerous.

"Mama would be sad if we quit," says Phoebe.

This is how Mirabel's face looks when Rosalyn and Phoebe and Old Mr. Jolly carry me into the kitchen: confused, like why isn't Charlie Anne up in the upper field with Anna May and Belle, and then mad, like a hornets' nest just fell on her head.

"What on earth happened?" she wants to know, pushing the flannel cloth I have picked for my new underpants (no rooster) onto the chair, and Old Mr. Jolly sets me down. Then I have to listen to Rosalyn tell her how we went and cleaned up the school all afternoon.

"She was supposed to be with the cows," says Mirabel, her voice all flat and hard, and Rosalyn looks at me and tells Mirabel how I had told her it was all right to go with them, and then I start moaning really loud to get everyone to forget how I haven't been too honest with anyone. Then Old Mr. Jolly winks at me.

"It was the oldest Thatcher boy," I say, sitting up.

Mirabel grabs a cloth from the drawer, dunks it into the boiling water on the cookstove, and pulls it up with a spoon. You can see the steam flying.

"No," I scream, "it's too hot!"

Mirabel pushes my arm away and starts dabbing,

and I am screaming because, all over again, it feels like shards of glass inside my head and then about a hundred angry knives against my cheek.

"Is that necessary?" Rosalyn asks, and Mirabel gives her the same icy look she gave me, and then Old Mr. Jolly clears his throat and says he better be on his way because he has some things he needs to be saying to the Thatchers.

"Wait," I say. "I have some things to say to the Thatchers. Phoebe and I will come."

Mirabel is making a paste of salt and flour. "You'll do no such thing," she says as she begins spreading it on my face. "You'll stay right here where I can keep an eye on you."

Then I am screaming so loud I forget all about how I wanted to go with Old Mr. Jolly in the first place.

"Why would that Thatcher boy do such a thing?" Mirabel asks as she brushes my hair into a ponytail and ties it up away from my face.

"Maybe he heard about the school and doesn't want it to open," Rosalyn says, reaching for Phoebe's hand. "Maybe the rock wasn't meant for Charlie Anne. We've been through this before."

Mirabel looks at Rosalyn and Phoebe. "Nonsense. We're not like that in these parts. We're neighborly."

"Then why don't you let me play with Phoebe?" The words jump out of me so fast I don't give any consideration to the consequences, as the manners book says I should. I am glad I say it, though, because next thing I know, Rosalyn raises her eyebrow at Mirabel and stares her flat in the face until Mirabel looks down.

Mirabel won't let me out of her sight for the next few days. She keeps putting a thin coat of molasses on my face so I won't bruise, and it turns out that I heal fast and I do not get a cheekful of pus.

She reads to me every night from the manners book:

> There is a defect in the character
> of any young girl who will go
> around with buttonless or half-
> buttoned shoes, with unmended
> rents in her dress and uncared-for
> hair, teeth and fingernails.
> Especially offensive to refined
> taste are spots or stains suggestive
> of lack of napkins at table or of
> aprons when they should be
> worn.

I roll my eyes. Then Mirabel makes Ivy make me vinegar tea: one tablespoon vinegar, one tablespoon sugar, a cup of boiling water.

When my stomach's upset from all the vinegar, she makes Ivy go out and pick some peppermint from the garden and steep me a cup of mint tea.

"Tea, tea, tea," complains Ivy. "How much tea does one person need?"

"A lot," I tell her.

"My goodness," Mirabel complains when she sees Rosalyn and Phoebe and Old Mr. Jolly coming across the road, "here they come again." But by the time they are on the porch, she already has water on for more tea. The curtains blowing at the window are mended and clean (thanks to Mirabel) and the table has a fresh cloth on top (thanks to Birdie). All the dishes are washed and stacked in the drainer and drying (thanks to Ivy, because Mirabel has noticed she hasn't been doing enough chores). The floor is scrubbed (thanks to Mirabel), and there is another vinegar pie just out of the oven (thanks to me).

Mirabel cuts big chunks of pie and puts them on the table. Birdie hurries in from where she's been playing down by the clothesline and goes over and climbs onto Phoebe's lap. Mirabel turns a little red. "Get off of there, Birdie."

"It's all right," Phoebe says, letting Birdie steal a piece of her pie.

"They like each other," I say, taking a bite of pie so big my cheeks fill out like an old hornpout.

Mirabel stands there, not sure what to do. "Don't fill your mouth so full, Charlie Anne," she says, finally, and sits down. "Where are your manners?" I wonder if she has ever eaten at a table with a colored girl before. I wonder if she knows about drinking fountains and white-people library books.

"I couldn't get past the oldest Thatcher boy to see the mother," Old Mr. Jolly is saying.

"Once a snake, always a snake," I tell him, cramming another piece of pie into my mouth.

"I've been thinking about bringing food to the Morrell family," Rosalyn says, looking at Mirabel. "Would you help me?"

Even before Mirabel answers, Rosalyn is rolling ahead with her next idea. "Phoebe has been wanting to learn how to make one of these vinegar pies. Perhaps she could come over and you could teach her how, Charlie Anne?"

I am nodding even before I see Mirabel's frowning face. As easy as pie, Rosalyn has found a way for Phoebe to come back.

"Phoebe, come see my room," I say, stuffing the last bite of pie in my mouth, and we are all running upstairs before Mirabel has a chance to do anything.

We fly onto our bed, and the feathers in the mattress sack are fluffed high because I just shook it out this morning. Everything is clean, the floor is swept, the window is washed.

"You all sleep in this bed?"

"Yes," says Birdie, giggling. "But Charlie Anne snores and keeps me awake all night."

"I do not," I say, jumping up and pouncing on her. "Take it back."

"No," she says, squealing, her arms all pinned. "Charlie Anne snores louder than Papa," she says before I can get my hand over her mouth, and then we are all shrieking and rolling around the bed, and pretty soon Mirabel is banging the top of the broom handle against the ceiling, which means quit it, or else.

"We need to do something to that Thatcher boy, to get him back," I say, rolling over on my stomach and propping my head up with my arms.

"What should we do?" Birdie asks, her eyes big.

"I don't know," I say. "Something that teaches him good." I watch a cow fly buzzing around our ceiling and remember the time the oldest Thatcher boy grabbed me on the walk after school and pulled me down in the dirt. "Eat it," he said, pushing a fistful of gravel into my mouth, making me gag until I kicked him good.

"Maybe make him eat dirt. Something like that."

Birdie looks a little doubtful. Phoebe looks a little doubtful. I feel a little doubtful.

"He's awful big," says Birdie.

"Maybe," says Phoebe, "the way to get him back is to get the school open and show him we're no quitters. That's what my mama would tell us."

Birdie and I just look at each other. You've got to hand it to Phoebe. She knows what she's talking about.

When we come down, they are still sitting around the table, and Mirabel is brewing more tea. Rosalyn is saying she'd like to hear some of that manners book she's been hearing so much about, and Mirabel takes it out of her pocket, and wouldn't you know it, the section Mirabel reads actually makes a teeny bit of sense:

> In all social relations, strive to
> throw your influence for that
> which is faithful, sincere, kind,
> generous, and just. Have a special
> thought and regard for those who
> may labor under disadvantages; be
> especially kind to the shrinking
> and timid, to the poor and
> unfortunate.

Mirabel pauses, and looks at Rosalyn. "I don't know why Charlie Anne makes such a fuss about this book all the time."

Rosalyn sips her tea and looks over at me. "Maybe girls should be a little noisy now and again, don't you think? Otherwise, bullies like that Thatcher boy can do whatever they want."

"This is how you make a vinegar pie," I am telling Phoebe.

Mirabel is peeling potatoes. "Did you know vinegar pie makes the hard times better?" she asks Phoebe in her loud voice. I've noticed she uses this voice all the time for Phoebe, like maybe Phoebe can't hear right or is a little slow-witted or something. Even my feet are embarrassed.

Phoebe's got that ironing board down her back again. "My mama knew how to make things better, but not by baking pies."

You can tell Mirabel doesn't know what to say to that. She goes back to the cookstove and stirs the beans for a long time, even though we all know beans don't need much stirring.

When the pies are in the oven, Mirabel shoos us outside, and Phoebe and I go sit on the porch. We watch Birdie run down through the sheets and look for something, then go back and sit by the shade of the barn, only to run back down again. She does it three times while we are sitting there.

"What's she doing?" Phoebe shields her eyes with her hand to block the sun.

I shrug. "Let's go see." And then Phoebe and I go down to find out.

"What are you looking for, Birdie?"

Birdie is hunting between the sheets, snapping them off their clothespins. Her cheeks are covered with tears. She goes back to searching.

"What is it, Birdie? What are you looking for?"

Birdie looks behind the last sheet, pulling it down on the ground. "I keep seeing Mama," she sobs. "But by the time I get down here, she's gone."

"Oh, Birdie," I say, getting down on my knees so I can look in her face. "Oh, Birdie."

I hold her and she cries my arm all wet. She looks up, sniffling. "Is Mama coming back, Charlie Anne?"

"I don't know, Birdie."

"If we wait long enough?"

"I don't know. Maybe in different ways from what we had before. You look just like her, you know."

"I do?"

"Yes," I say, hugging her, and then Phoebe is there, too, looking like she knows all about losing your mama. Then we pick up the sheets and brush them off and hang them back up again. Anna May is telling me to thank heaven that it is not a muddy day.

When we walk up to the house, we do it just the

way Old Mr. Jolly and Rosalyn do it with Phoebe: we both take one of Birdie's hands and we swing her up off the ground with every few steps and pretty soon she is shrieking and laughing and the tears that are clinging to her lashes from before are wondering what they're still doing there.

That night I let Birdie sleep close to me and I don't make her push over.

"Charlie Anne?"

"Yes, Birdie?"

"You spoil me with hugs. Just like Mama."

The Morrell house is very dark when we get there. The door is shut up tight and the curtains are drawn. There is no smoke coming out of the chimney and even the chickens are still.

I am ready for Old Mr. Jolly to fly Phoebe and me out of the back of the truck, but he is already hurrying up the walk and knocking on the door, and Rosalyn is right behind him. Mirabel is carrying the basket of food: golden harvest soup, apple dumplings, her pot of baked beans and a vinegar pie made by Phoebe and me.

Pumpkins and squash are still sitting in the garden, and if somebody doesn't come get them pretty soon, they'll be good for nothing but the compost pile. There's no rooster, no dog, no cats running around. When Old Mr. Jolly knocks again, I see a curtain move.

"Knock harder," says Mirabel.

I go over and tap on the window. It is icy cold. "Sarah, it's me, Charlie Anne. We brought food and stuff. Open the door. Please."

Finally, after about a hundred years, the door opens just a sliver. Sarah Morrell looks out. Her eyes are big as Anna May's.

"How you doing, Sarah?" I step closer. "We've got a big basket of things for you."

She looks unsure if she should open the door any more. "My mama is sick."

We are all just looking at Sarah. Her dress is hanging off her shoulders and she has no shoes and no socks.

"There's apple dumplings in the basket Mirabel is carrying," I say softly. "Can we come in and see your mama?"

Sarah gives me a long look and then steps out of the way so we can all go in together. The house is dark and cold, and there is a lump of blankets on the couch and there are two little girls standing near the table, which is covered with dishes. There is a bad smell coming from the kitchen.

"Oh my," says Mirabel. "Bring me those dishes," she says, pointing to the dirty plates, and she rushes off to the kitchen.

Old Mr. Jolly and Rosalyn go right over and kneel in front of Mrs. Morrell and ask how she is and she tries to smile, but she winces and whispers how she has surely seen better days. Old Mr. Jolly goes out and gets a big bucket of fresh water from the well, and Rosalyn squeezes out a cloth and starts wiping Mrs. Morrell's face, and then Mrs. Morrell is crying.

It is a sad thing to see someone's mama crying. Phoebe and I just stand there not knowing what to do, and then Rosalyn looks over and says maybe we can lay out the food. Mirabel gives us a towel, and Phoebe and I wipe off the table and start unloading everything. We tell Sarah to get plates and forks, and I show her and the little girls how to put the forks on the left, and napkins under, and I tell myself to stop it because I'm sounding like Mirabel. Then we watch the Morrell girls all plow through the apple dumplings (it's okay to have dessert first sometimes, Rosalyn says), and then they reach for the pie. Mirabel washes some bowls and some spoons and I ladle out the soup.

Rosalyn helps Mrs. Morrell with her soup, but she has to stop because Mrs. Morrell has started crying again. Rosalyn dabs at Mrs. Morrell's eyes with a napkin and keeps saying, "There, there, things will get better very soon. You'll see." Old Mr. Jolly jumps up and hurries outside, and he brings in wood and starts a fire in the cookstove, and then he carries in bucket after bucket of water, and by the time Mirabel has heated it almost to boiling, Mrs. Morrell has stopped crying.

Sarah shows us where the broom is and the washbucket and the mops, and Phoebe and I and Rosalyn get to work helping Mirabel, all of us cleaning and scrubbing and putting everything away, and while we are doing that, we tell the girls all about the school.

Rosalyn asks Mrs. Morrell if maybe the girls could go to school tomorrow, and by the time we get the house clean and warmed with a fire, she is saying that maybe they could.

"Can Charlie Anne come, too?" Phoebe asks Mirabel, and then everyone is looking at Mirabel.

Mirabel twists a towel around her fingers. "Gosh, it's getting hot in here," she says. Then she opens all the windows to let some fresh air in.

The oldest Thatcher boy is chopping wood by the barn, and he looks up as we pull into the driveway. He isn't wearing a coat, and he has that mean look he's had since his father got killed in that hunting accident.

This was Old Mr. Jolly's idea, to bring food over. Maybe he could get to the mother and talk to her about her oldest son, he told us.

Old Mr. Jolly turns off the truck, and we watch big dogs on chains howl and jump toward us, and I think on how you'd have to be crazy as a loon to get out of the truck.

The house is turned gable-face to the road, which means the front door looks out on a field overgrown with ragweed and thistle. The side door is covered with poison ivy. Three doghouses sit on the grass and the clothesline creaks around and around. Paint is peeling and cracking off every single clapboard.

After a while, the oldest Thatcher boy comes over to the truck, an ax over his shoulder. Two other boys come out of the house and watch us. No one is wearing shoes.

"What do you want?"

Old Mr. Jolly opens the truck and climbs out and slowly straightens his back. He is tall, now that Rosalyn makes him stand up straight. "We brought some things over. We hear your mother is sick."

The boy backs up a pace. "We don't need no help."

"We know you and your brothers are fine," Old Mr. Jolly says, pointing to the porch, where there are now four boys standing beside a broken swing. "We brought food for your mother. How is she?"

"Poorly," he says. "She has the influenza." The boy is stubbing his toe into the dirt.

"Well, she might like this," says Rosalyn, climbing out of the other side of the truck, carrying a basket, keeping her eye on the dogs. "There's soup and bread and apple dumplings and pie."

Rosalyn holds out the basket. "Can we go up and see your mother?"

"She don't like company." The boy scratches his toe in the dirt again.

Rosalyn watches the dogs. "I can see that."

Mirabel climbs out of the truck. I watch her noticing the dirt all over the boy's neck and his ripped shirt and dirty feet.

Rosalyn takes a step closer and sets the basket in front of him. "We're opening the school tomorrow, if you'd like to come."

I look at Phoebe, my mouth open. "NO!" I can't

believe Rosalyn is inviting the oldest Thatcher boy. I remember how he stuck my braid in the inkwell on my desk, and how Miss Moran thought I had done it myself to get attention. "NO!" I say again.

The oldest Thatcher boy turns and looks at Phoebe and me. I look right back at him, daring him to look away first.

"Is she going?" he asks, pointing to Phoebe.

"Yes," says Rosalyn, her voice slow and careful. "The school is for everyone."

"I ain't going to no colored school."

No rock is necessary this time. The words cut Phoebe all by themselves. Then he picks the basket up off the ground and walks to the porch and tells his brothers to get in the house now or he will beat them silly, and then he follows them inside and slams the door.

We notice the garbage all over the porch, and then Mirabel marches after the Thatcher boys. Old Mr. Jolly starts after her. We'll just see about that, I tell my feet, and I am hurrying right behind.

It smells like cats, many, many cats that don't have the sense to pee outside. Blankets are nailed over the windows to keep the sun out.

"Where's your mother?" Mirabel asks, and the little one points to the bedroom.

"Ma'am?" says Mirabel, going in. "Mrs. Thatcher?"

Mirabel is right over, pulling the blankets down and opening the windows so she can see better. The bedroom is not much bigger than our pantry. Mrs. Thatcher has only a sheet covering her, and she shivers when the fresh air comes pouring in the room.

Mirabel turns to us. "This is going on right under our noses? My goodness."

"You," she says to one of the middle boys. "Go get some fresh water. And you," she says to another, "go put on some tea. And somebody get a mop, for God's sake, and clean this room up."

Mirabel forgets all about her manners book and orders us all around for the next couple of hours. When we are done, Mrs. Thatcher is eating a piece of vinegar pie and sipping some strong tea. Mirabel has written down chores for all the boys to do. "I'm coming back tomorrow to make sure these things are done."

"They can't read," I whisper to her. Mirabel looks at Rosalyn, and turns a little red. Then she reads the list. "Make sure all the cats stay out of the house. That's number one."

As we are leaving, Mirabel turns to the oldest Thatcher boy. "My girls are going to school tomorrow. And if you try to stop them, you'll have me to answer to. Do you understand?"

I feel my heart lighten, just listening to Mirabel say

that. I wonder when she changed her mind about the school. The littlest boy is nodding, up and down, up and down. The oldest Thatcher boy is giving me an ugly look. I know things are not over.

When we get back, Old Mr. Jolly says he has been wanting to fix that swing of mine for some time now and he needs something to do to keep his mind off things and would that be all right and I say yes, yes, it surely would.

Well. When we are done getting the ropes up to the highest limb that can hold me, I swing farther than I ever have before, almost all the way up to where Mama is, and she is laughing, she is so happy for me.

I tell her I am still too mad to talk to her and she says that's okay. Sometimes that's the way things are when mamas die. Sometimes there are a lot of mad feelings that need working out.

I believe my bed wants me to stay, and it starts humming that happy tune that makes me feel better about things, but I am very stern with it this morning and tell it that no, today I am going back to school, where Rosalyn knows how to help readers like me.

I put my feet on the cold floorboards, and my toes are so happy they don't even notice. I give Birdie a hurry-up–get-up kiss on the cheek, and she hollers to be entering the wake-up world so early, and I yell at Ivy to get up or she will sleep right through this amazing, wonderful day.

Ivy rolls over and sticks her head under the pillow, but I am already jumping into my sunflower trousers. A girl who is going to school can pick out what she wants to wear, Mirabel or no Mirabel. Then I rush down the stairs and out the door to Belle and Anna May.

It is so early the sun's not even up and I hear the trees along the road waking each other. They tell the stone wall not to grumble so much about standing still. Being strong is no small thing, they say, and they are right, but I am glad for my feet and how they can fly out to the barn.

Olympia and Minnie and Bea still have their heads tucked under their wings, and Anna May wants to know what I am doing here looking for milk so early. Belle is wondering what the dickens is going on.

"Oh, happy day!" I yell over to Minnie and Olympia and Bea, and they look up and start clucking about being woken up, and then I reach around and give Anna May a big hug, and then I go get the milk pail and the stool and put it down beside her and tell her she better be good, or else. I don't have time for any fooling around.

Anna May turns around and gives me one of her grumpy looks. "Oh, don't you be doing that," I tell her, and when I get the pail nearly full of milk and am thinking about being with Phoebe at school and how I'm going to learn to read so well that even Becky Ellis can't laugh, that's when Anna May lets her kicking foot fly and she sends the bucket straight up in the air and the milk comes flying down all over me and my new trousers.

I do more than give Anna May my most terrible mad look. I give her a you-know-what on the backside.

"They aren't so bad. I will wear them anyway," I am telling Mirabel.

"You will not wear soaking wet trousers to school. You can wear your dress." Mirabel is fixing twice as many biscuits as usual because she's taking some over to the Thatchers to make sure they have done their chores.

"I don't want to wear that dress," I wail. My bright yellow trousers are stuck to my legs and Ivy is laughing. She is eating biscuits, and Birdie is only eating the blackberry jam. Ivy and Birdie are wearing the made-over dresses that Mirabel made, purple as pansies and decorated with ribbon and lace that Mrs. Ellis sent over.

I cross my arms over my chest and just stand there in the middle of the kitchen, dripping, smelling potatoes boil and thinking how mad I am at Anna May.

"Remember what we read last night?" Mirabel says, looking over at me, a frown already on her face. "Remember what you are to do when you are angry?"

I remember.

> If you will learn to be silent and
> not speak at all when you feel
> that your temper is getting or has
> gotten the better of you, you will
> soon get the better of your
> temper.
>
> ❧

I do not think this is easy when Ivy is laughing at you and your trousers are sticking to you like butter on bread.

* * *

I believe my trousers want to go to school. They are unhappy that Mirabel is making me hang them on the line. I am very firm with them and say how they mustn't be mad at me. Blame Anna May, or even better, blame Mirabel. She's the one making me wear this pea green made-over dress that is so big it reaches down and touches the top of my shoes.

Mama whispers softly that it will be all right. No one will care about what I am wearing, especially not Rosalyn. Mama says wait till I see what Old Mr. Jolly has done with the woodshed.

What? I ask, starting to tremble.

Don't worry, Charlie Anne. He's filling it with wood, not children. Hurry, or you'll be late.

It takes Ivy about a hundred more minutes to get her hair pinned just right. Then I take Birdie's hand and tell her we are going to wait by the road for Phoebe, and Birdie keeps asking me if we will get lemon drops. She doesn't understand that school isn't the place for lemon drops. It's the place for reading.

When Phoebe comes out of her house with Rosalyn, they are both wearing bright yellow trousers.

"Where are yours?" Phoebe wants to know, and I point to the clothesline and my dripping pair of pants.

"Oh," says Phoebe, and Rosalyn tells me she thinks

I look just wonderful in my pea green dress, and after that I feel much better.

Ivy keeps looking over her shoulder to see if Becky is coming, but I tell her she must be forgetting about how Mrs. Ellis wanted a teacher from Boston.

"She won't be coming, will she?" I ask Rosalyn, and Rosalyn puts her lips in a straight line, just like Papa.

"No, I don't think she will. Maybe some other day. People have a way of changing if you wait long enough."

Rosalyn is carrying a stack of books, and I see *David Copperfield* on top, and I say to myself, Good, I've been wondering how things turn out for poor little David.

She tells us Old Mr. Jolly has gone on ahead to check on the school and to get a fire started in the woodstove. Then she gives me a map of the United States to carry and also an American flag. I am so proud to be going to school with Phoebe. We walk arm in arm.

Rosalyn starts humming a tune I've never heard before, and by the time we are out of sight of the house, she puts words to the music:

> *Bright morning stars are rising,*
> *Bright morning stars are rising,*
> *Bright morning stars are rising,*
> *Day is a-breaking in my soul.*

Then Phoebe starts, her voice flying straight up to heaven:

> *Oh, where are our dear mothers,*
> *Day is a-breaking in my soul.*
> *They've gone to heaven a-shouting,*
> *Day is a-breaking in my soul.*

And then I open my mouth and try and sing the chorus without sounding too much like a toad croaking:

> *Bright morning stars are rising,*
> *Bright morning stars are rising,*
> *Bright morning stars are rising,*
> *Day is a-breaking in my soul.*

Then Birdie starts singing, her voice all soft, and I think about how it's been a long time since I have been so happy as I am now.

40

When we get around the corner, there are three dead robins lined up in a row across the road. Birdie shrieks and starts wailing and I have to pick her up and my stomach starts balling up. Rosalyn looks quickly all around us and then tells us we better hurry, and I put Birdie down and tell her we all have to run.

I wonder why there is no wood-smoke smell in the air. When we get around the corner, I see why. Old Mr. Jolly hasn't even gotten inside the school to start the fire. Instead, he is ripping off a bunch of old boards that someone nailed right across the school door.

"Oh, no," says Rosalyn.

"Whoever did this took a lot of time," Old Mr. Jolly is saying. "There are a lot of boards here."

Rosalyn reaches for Phoebe, and together they look at everything blocking our way. Birdie won't let me go.

"I won't quit," Rosalyn keeps telling Old Mr. Jolly.

"Then let's get the rest of these boards off," he says, and he gives us all tools from the back of his truck: hammers, screwdrivers, even a crowbar. It takes us a whole hour to get the boards off and broken up, and Old Mr. Jolly tells us we should use them to start the fire for our soup.

When the fire is catching and we are all calming down, I ask Old Mr. Jolly who he thinks did such a thing, and if he thinks it was the oldest Thatcher boy, and he says there's no way of knowing for sure. "And the dead robins," says Birdie, starting to howl again.

I lift her up and wipe her tears with my hand and catch Old Mr. Jolly looking into Rosalyn's face and running his fingers through her hummingbird hair.

"I think I'll just stay here today, doing some chores outside, while you hold school. And I think you should lock the door."

She nods and he goes out to the woodshed, and a few minutes later we hear him chopping wood.

"First thing we have to do each morning is get the soup going," Rosalyn says, and we are soon chopping potatoes and onions and turnips and carrots. Ivy is complaining she doesn't like turnip.

"It sweetens up once it's cooked. You'll be surprised how a thing can change," Rosalyn says, and Ivy doesn't look too sure about that, and I notice she has the *Movie Mirror* magazine tucked into her pocket.

Soon the schoolhouse is warm from the fire and smelling good from the golden harvest soup, and we can hear Old Mr. Jolly outside chopping wood. Rosalyn tells me I can sit near Phoebe—for a little while, until we start reading and she starts needing to be assistant teacher.

Birdie sits beside me on the other side and Ivy sits behind us. Then we wait for the other children to come, and Rosalyn keeps looking at the door.

Ivy is slumped in her seat whispering how she told me so, how nobody is going to come to this stupid school and how she is going straight home to tell Mirabel we should have waited for the teacher from Boston.

"Shut up, Ivy. Will you just shut up?"

"Perhaps we should start reading?" Rosalyn asks.

I say that might be a very good idea, and it comes out all mad because my temper is short from the worry over the robins and the boards on the door and from waiting for more children to show up.

Rosalyn reaches for *David Copperfield* and asks if I would mind if she started from the beginning since neither Ivy nor Birdie has heard it, and I say that would be okay, since I like the beginning very much.

Old Mr. Jolly comes in and dumps a big load of wood in the wood box and then Rosalyn opens the book.

> Whether I shall turn out to be
> the hero of my own life, or
> whether that station will be held
> by anybody else, these pages
> must show.

Her voice is soft and the fire is warm, and as I listen to the story, I start to forget about the boards nailed across the door, and I start feeling all wrapped up in Mama's poppy-colored quilt, and if I weren't feeling so bad about David Copperfield's sad life, sadder than even mine, I could fall asleep. After a while, I turn around to make sure Ivy isn't reading her *Movie Mirror*, and even her eyes are wet from the sadness of what Mr. Murdstone is doing to little David. Rosalyn is just getting to the part where David gets sent to the tiny wretched bedroom at the top of the stairs when she sets the book down.

"I just want to remind all you teary eyes out there that this is the beginning of the book and things have a way of turning around. That's just the way books are. You have to keep being hopeful when things are bad. Do you understand that?"

I look at Phoebe. Tears are falling down her face. I reach over and squeeze her hand.

Rosalyn waits to make sure we really do understand, and that we are nodding—yes, yes, we understand—before she picks up where she left off. Then she puts the book down again, and I groan way down deep inside myself because I want her to keep going something awful.

"And sometimes," she says, "it is a good idea to read about someone who's having trouble—maybe more trouble than we are—because it helps us find ways through our own troubles."

Yes, yes, even Birdie is nodding. Then Rosalyn picks up the book again, and just as I begin to think that David is about as sorry a little creature as ever lived, there is a rap at the door.

4 1

Well. My seat is telling me to sit right where I am and not move. Phoebe has that ironing board down her back again, and I know she's thinking what I'm thinking: whoever nailed up all that wood over the door is waiting out there now, ready to do something even worse.

Birdie jumps into my lap. "Shh," I say, rubbing my hands over her hair. "Where are your lemon drops?"

She holds up her last sliver.

"I told you we should have never come," Ivy is saying. "What if it's that Thatcher boy?"

"He has cooties," says Birdie.

Rosalyn closes the book and looks at us. "Girls, we are not afraid, are we?" She is looking like she's not fearful of anything, not even bats flying around a schoolhouse. You can hear Old Mr. Jolly chopping wood out back. He must not know anyone is out front. "Charlie Anne," she says, "would you please answer the door?"

Well. We all just sit there. I feel the hundred knives slashing at my cheek. I shake my head.

"There's no need to be afraid," Rosalyn says gently.

"Stand up, Charlie Anne, walk tall, and open the door so we can greet whoever would like to join us."

"But the boards . . ."

"Someone who did something like that won't come out in the daylight. That sort of thing is done at night. We don't need to be afraid."

We hear more raps at the door. "Charlie Anne," says Rosalyn.

I turn to Phoebe. "Come with me." Her eyes are moons, filling up her whole face, and she shakes her head.

"We are blood sisters, remember?" I say. Phoebe shakes her head. No.

"That's a good idea," says Rosalyn. "Phoebe, go help."

When I take Phoebe's hand, her fingers are shaking and cold. I tell Birdie she has to get off my lap, but she won't let go of my leg, so finally, we walk to the door, Phoebe, me, and me dragging Birdie.

I grab the handle and look back at Rosalyn. She smiles and nods and I open the door.

The first thing I see are the barn boots, three sizes too big, stuffed with rags no doubt, and the flour-sack dresses.

Then I notice that the dresses are clean and pressed and the boots are spotless. It is the Morrell girls: Sarah, Deborah and Mary. Their hair is all washed and brushed, and when Sarah gives me a basketful of biscuits, I see her fingernails are clean. I tell myself to stop it. I am acting just like Mirabel.

"Come in, oh, come in, girls!" says Rosalyn, jumping up, and I am breathing a very large sigh of relief, and I check to see if Phoebe is sighing, too, and she is.

Rosalyn says we are going to have a school like no other, a wonderful school, where we will grow readers, and then she tells the Morrell girls to find seats, and then Rosalyn tells us she has some things she needs to go over.

"First, everyone who can should bring something to put into our soup pot. Even an onion is fine. Each day we'll make a soup for lunch." Rosalyn walks over and lifts the cover off the pot and stirs the soup, and the smell spreads all through the school, and I have to tell my belly it has to wait just a little while longer.

"Next," Rosalyn says, "we're going to start the day discussing history and geography and the world around us because I think it's important to know why things are the way they are.

"For example, we could begin by talking about the hard times we are living in right now. Charlie Anne, Ivy, Birdie, I know your father has gone north to build roads to make money to keep the farm. And hasn't Mr. Morrell done the same thing?"

All three Morrell girls nod.

"And our brothers, too," says Sarah.

I think about Peter. I wonder if school in Boston is better than this. I look around the cozy little room, with the sun pouring through the shining windows, and I don't see how it could be.

"Does anyone know what President Roosevelt meant when he said, 'There is nothing to fear but fear itself'?"

No one says anything. Birdie puts the last of her lemon drop in her mouth.

"I think he means that if we can't see the good in life, it will be hard to turn the tough things around. What do you think?"

No one says anything.

"Well, what are you all doing at home to get by?" Rosalyn asks.

"Vinegar pie," says Ivy, pinching her nose, and I want to smack her.

"Handing-me-down-forevers," I say.

"Not enough lemon drops," says Birdie.

"That's right," says Rosalyn. "Sometimes, though, doing without makes people bitter. And sometimes, instead of seeing the wonder of another person, all they see are the differences."

"Like with Phoebe?" asks Birdie.

"Yes," says Rosalyn. "Like with Phoebe." She reaches over and takes Phoebe's hand and then I reach over and take her other hand and we all watch Phoebe's eyes fill up with tears. We can tell she doesn't want to talk about it, so we don't press her with a lot of questions. Sometimes you just have to let somebody be.

Then it is time for reading.

Rosalyn says she's going to call each of us up and read with us alone. Then the ones who are done will go with Phoebe for some extra reading help if they need it.

She hands out some paper and says that while we are waiting, we can write about how we are getting by during these hard times we are living in, and if our writing is not ready for that, we can draw a picture.

"I will love your work, no matter which you choose," she says.

I start drawing a vinegar pie. It is my best ever, with a high fluted crust and steam rising out of it, and right beside it I draw all the ingredients: butter, three eggs, vinegar, vanilla and sugar.

All the time I am drawing, I am thinking about the spot under the teacher's desk and I'm wondering what Old Mr. Jolly has done about the woodshed.

Rosalyn goes oldest to youngest, so Ivy gets called up first. Ivy reads a page from *First Reader*, then Rosalyn says my goodness, you are ready for *Second Reader*. I have that sinking feeling as Rosalyn hands it to Ivy. She is like a plow horse, pushing through row after row of words, without ever tiring at all.

You can see Rosalyn getting all excited, and she hands Ivy *Third Reader*. "I had no idea you were such a good reader, Ivy."

Then she tells Ivy to read a poem called "Hiawatha's Childhood," and Ivy reads the whole thing, even the funny Indian words I have never heard before.

Rosalyn is smiling like she just got a secret present and she tells Ivy good job and good job again and now she can go back to her seat.

And then Rosalyn says it's my turn.

I shake my head, because now my hands are sweating and my stomach is flipping upside down. Rosalyn giggles, which is not the response I am expecting at all, and she comes over and puts her hand out. "You have nothing to be afraid of."

Well. I do so have something to be afraid of. That's the thing.

Rosalyn takes my hand and leads me up front and hands me *First Reader* and asks me what the letters are on the first page.

The letters are jumping again like corn popping, just like they did with Miss Moran. I squint my eyes and stumble. I see all the *d*s and *b*s and can't figure out which is which. The blackboard is giving me comforting looks. It is not very helpful, though, and all I can think about is how good of a reader Ivy is.

Rosalyn takes my hand and squeezes it. "It's okay, Charlie Anne. I'll show you a trick. Do you know your left from your right?"

"Yes," I say, thanking heaven that I milk Anna May on her right side, morning and night.

"Good," says Rosalyn. "Now make a fist with your left hand, like this. Now put your thumb up."

I do what she says.

"That is a *b*. See how it has a belly sticking out?"

I nod, feeling a little like a baby, hoping Phoebe can't see.

"Excellent. Now, do the same thing with your right hand. That is a *d*. Now, let's write the word *b-e-d*. See how it makes a little headboard, mattress and footboard? Bed starts *b-b-b* with *b*, so you always know which way the belly points."

I make a little bed, just like she says. "Like this?"

"Yes," she says, pulling me close so she can whisper in my ear: "This trick never, ever fails."

"Never?"

"Never."

Someone should have told me how assistant teachers are pretty bossy.

Since the sun is out and it is getting warm, and Old Mr. Jolly is nearby, Rosalyn tells Sarah and Birdie and me that we can go under the maple trees. Phoebe brings a basket of books. I think, now that I know my *b–d* trick, I am ready for *First Reader*, at least.

"Don't you want to practice?" Phoebe asks.

"No. I can do it." I'm a little hurt that she thinks I need so much help.

"*Pat, doll, cat, ball, gill, hot, moon,*" I say, opening the first page.

Phoebe has a puzzled look on her face. "You're not sounding these words out, Charlie Anne." She looks over my shoulder. "You got some of them right but most of them wrong. They are *pot, ball, cat, doll, girl, hat, moon.*"

I pull the book back, making a tiny tear in the page.

Phoebe is looking like she's wondering what's gotten into me, and she says there are many confusing words that she wants to practice with me, and I say okay, but when can we get to the reading, and she says, "Charlie Anne."

I want to tell her right then and there that she is sounding rather like a know-it-all, but I bite my tongue because I remember that manners book and also because I want to be reading so much—much more than I want to make her mad.

"There are some words that can get us all mixed up. Especially when they are the same word that means two different things. Like *bear*," says Phoebe.

I am tapping my thumb on my leg. Tap. Tap. Tap.

"Sometimes it means a big black bear and sometimes it means trying to hold up a big load. Like a foundation holding up a house."

Phoebe shows the word to Birdie. "See? They are the same word."

I am cracking my knuckles. Crack. Crack. Crack.

"Do you see, Charlie Anne?"

"I know all this already." I am rolling my eyes. Roll. Roll. Roll.

Then Phoebe points to the word *left*. "Sometimes it is a direction, like you put your fork on the left." She's starting to sound just like Mirabel.

"And then," says Phoebe, "sometimes it means Mama left me."

Then Phoebe wants to tell us a story about her

mama, and I tell her that is very nice and all but when are we going to get to reading?

She looks annoyed. "Charlie Anne, who is the teacher here?"

I want to tell her, I am feeling mighty sorry right now that it is you, but I don't because I want to get to reading more than I want to do anything, even eat lunch. Plus Mirabel's dumb little manners book keeps reminding me that I will be losing love and friends if I don't watch myself. I don't want to lose Phoebe, but I do want her to get to the reading.

Then Sarah wants a turn and Phoebe gives her *First Reader* and she is so good she jumps right to *Second Reader* and I am feeling all terrible again that I'll never be as good a reader as anyone else.

Then Birdie wants to know how did Phoebe learn to sing so good, and then we have to hear the whole long story about how her mama told her there was a light inside her and she had a choice: either she could be who she was supposed to be, or she could be a quitter.

"Wasn't that supposed to be a secret just for me?" I want to know.

Phoebe looks at me very sternly. I feel like I am Anna May being looked at.

"What's wrong with you?" she wants to know. "It's just Birdie."

I don't know what's wrong. I give her my most terrible mad look and I'm not even sure exactly why, but right then and there, under that big maple tree, I change my mind about what I told Anna May and Belle: how nothing can tear blood sisters apart.

43

I ignore the candle Phoebe lights in her window that night, and for the next four days, I tell Mirabel I have a bellyache so bad that I can't eat and I can't drink and I need the hot-water bottle, and she tells me to stay in bed. I think as I hear Ivy and Birdie get ready for school that there has never been a girl as pitiful as me.

Rosalyn comes over to check on me one afternoon, but I tell Mirabel I am too sick to talk to her, and I don't want to talk to Phoebe, either. Especially not Phoebe.

"You are just a faker," Ivy says, coming in with more peppermint tea.

"I am not," I say, being careful not to sit up too fast or to look too hopeful that there might be cookies with the tea.

I hear Anna May and Belle wondering what the dickens I'm doing, anyway, and how come Mirabel is coming out with the milk pail.

On Saturday, since there's no school anyway, I tell myself I might as well get up, and I tell Mirabel I am feeling better and head out for my swing. I ask Anna May and Belle if I look like a bolt of lightning as I soar through the sky and they tell me I do.

I swing and swing and swing on the swing Old Mr. Jolly fixed so fine, and I get myself going higher, higher, higher. I practice pointing my toes up and waving my arm out to the side, just like Phoebe does. Then I lean over backward and let my hair almost touch the ground, and I see Anna May and Belle wondering what I am doing all upside down like that, about to break my neck.

I keep watching for Phoebe so she will see that I am much better than she is at swinging, and then, after a very long time, she comes out her front door and notices me on my swing. She takes her swing into the barn, and I count to thirty so I know she is climbing up to the very top of her hayloft, and then she comes shooting out with her toes pointing up, and she leans over backward, and I think one of her every-which-way braids is actually touching the ground.

Well. I need to get higher so I can get a better start. As soon as Phoebe flies back to her hayloft, I climb off my swing and rush into my barn and come out dragging the apple barrel. I look over at Anna May and Belle. They have stopped munching and are watching me. Even Minnie and Olympia and Bea are looking to see what I am doing.

"I'll show you," I tell them, climbing to the top of the apple barrel, slipping just a little because it is not on solid ground, and I jump into my swing and I am flying up, up, up and I am laughing because Phoebe may read better than me, but I am the better swinger.

Then Phoebe comes shooting out of her barn again. Her toes are pointed up and she lets go, first one hand and then the other. Then when her swing goes as high as it can, she jumps and lands with a little roll. She stands, says "Ta-da" and curtsies.

Believe me, I don't even bother to clap. Instead, I look around for something higher to climb onto.

I look over at Belle. She's looking up at me, wondering what the dickens is taking me so long to figure things out. Why don't I climb up onto her back?

So I tell her to come on over, but she just stands there looking at me, munching on some grass, and I have to go over and get her. Now, climbing up on a cow is not the easiest thing, especially when you have a swing in your hand. For one thing, Belle won't hold still.

"Stop walking," I tell her.

The other problem is cows have such bony backs. Anna May is not so sure about things. She comes over for a closer look.

"Don't make Belle all skitters," I tell her, standing up, trying to keep my balance and jumping onto my swing.

But it works, and Belle bolts out of the way, and I fly. I tap my feet and do a little shuffle in the air with my new shoes, and then I notice that Phoebe is swinging even higher.

I let myself slow down and think about how I can go farther. I look up the trunk of the elm tree. I think about how if I could climb up there, I could jump out of the tree.

So, I wrap the ropes around my shoulders and start climbing. Birdie sees me and rushes over, whining, and crying that this time I really will go straight to heaven, and I tell her she has to stop doing this, and to shush, but she starts sobbing, and I tell her to stop being such a baby because Mirabel will hear. Birdie doesn't understand that when you are so mad at your best friend, you don't care if you break your neck or not. You just want her to know you are the best at swinging.

"You be quiet, Birdie," I yell down to her, but she is already running for the house.

As I climb higher, Phoebe shoots out of her barn, a golden bullet, and this time she opens her mouth and starts to sing, and just like all the other times, heaven comes out. She sings so beautifully that even Belle and Anna May pause to see who's making that wonderful sound.

"Stop looking at her," I tell them.

I open my mouth and start singing, too, and I sing the only song I know, "Amazing Grace, how sweet the sound." I am screaming and croaking and belting out the words, and when I look over, Phoebe seems in pain just to listen to me. Belle and Anna May walk away, and pretty soon Olympia, Minnie and Bea follow them, and I tell them all, go, good riddance, who needs friends anyway?

Two more feet and I am higher in the elm tree than I have ever been, and I sit myself on my swing and then I jump.

I feel myself fall, fall, fall, the earth coming close, and then the rope catches and I sail out, and then the swing catches me again, because swings are like that, and I am flying back the other way, straight back, and I try and twist myself around because when you're on a swing, you need to know where you are going.

And just for an instant, I see Anna May over by the privy looking at me with her molasses eyes, but they are not soft, they are filled with cow-worry.

Then I slam into the tree and feel myself crumple and my hands let go of the ropes, and I am falling to the ground, where the roots of the elm tree rise up in a gnarled and angry mess.

When I look up, there is Mirabel picking me up and carrying me into the house, and I am thankful she is pretty good with cuts because I have a lot of them.

44

All the next morning I sit on my swing and watch to see if Phoebe is looking for me. After a long time, she comes out and crosses the road and pretends she can't see me. She climbs over the fence and walks right up to Belle. I can hardly believe it.

"Did it hurt when Charlie Anne climbed up on you like that?" she says, kissing Belle all over the nose. "She doesn't know how to treat a cow, does she?"

I am off my swing like a bullet. "Don't you be touching Belle," I yell at her, rushing over. My cuts hurt quite a bit. "You stay away from her, do you hear?"

But she does touch her. She touches her all over and then she pats her all tenderly on her wet nose and whispers little soft words in her ear, just the way Belle likes it. Anna May comes rushing over to see what the dickens is going on and if maybe Phoebe has some corn in her pocket, or maybe an apple. Then Phoebe is giving little whispers in Anna May's ears, too. I think she is telling her bad things about me.

"Don't you be doing that. Don't you be saying things about me to Belle and Anna May."

"You don't need to worry about that," Phoebe says,

backing up from Belle and looking at me. "I'm not even *thinking* about you, Charlie Anne."

Well, that hurts just a little because I have been thinking about Phoebe ever since school, but I do not let her know that. Then Phoebe gives Belle and Anna May big goodbye hugs and sets off toward the river.

"Don't you dare go in our fields," I yell. "That river is ours. Plus it's too dangerous now."

"I know how to be careful of a river, Charlie Anne. Why are you acting all stupid?"

Well, that makes me so mad I run after her, a little slowly on account of my cuts, and I grab her arm and jerk her around to look at me. "I AM NOT MAD. AND STAY OUT OF OUR FIELDS."

Phoebe yanks herself out of my grip and she hisses, "Don't you ever touch me again, Charlie Anne."

All of a sudden I know exactly where she is headed. "Oh, no," I tell her. "Don't you dare go by my mama. I am not sharing her with you."

"I am not going by your mama. And when did God make you the owner of that river?"

That's the last thing Phoebe says before she turns away from me and stomps off into our fields, and I climb back on my swing and spend a whole long time swinging higher than Phoebe.

When I get tired of swinging and go in the house, Mirabel wants to know why I have been missing for so long, because she wants me to dump all the potato peels on the compost.

It is getting cold. The sheets I hung out are stiff. Mirabel will tell me soon to go get them and bring them back in, it's too cold, she'll say, and I will want to tell her why didn't she think of this before?

I am thinking about this when Mama starts calling, *Hurry, Charlie Anne, hurry.* I hear the river rushing over the big rocks that sit piggyback on each other out in the middle, and when it does, it makes a booming, booming, booming. I'm not talking to you, I tell her.

Hurry, Charlie Anne, hurry, she calls again, and I put the compost bucket on the ground and put my ear up to the wind. The river is loud from all the rain last night. *Hurry, Charlie Anne.*

I walk down by the clothesline and out past Anna May and Belle. Their eyes are filled with cow-worry. I climb over the fence and through the garden, now all picked over, and start along the way that Phoebe went, out through the cornfield with all the corn cut down. *Hurry, Charlie Anne, hurry,* and now Mama is screaming and the river is screaming, too, and I've never heard either of them do this before, and I begin to run.

I fly over corn stubble, listening to the water pound. I call out to Mama, and when I reach her, the river is racing like there's no tomorrow and I ask Mama what is wrong, and she says, *Phoebe.*

I do not see anything except churning, rushing

water. My heart pounds. I hurry downriver where the beech trees are all silvery with yellow leaves, and I look out and keep asking Mama where is Phoebe, but now that I am so close to the river, all I hear is the roaring.

I don't know what you're saying! I yell back to Mama, and I rush up the ridge that towers over the water and go by Mama.

Hurry, Charlie Anne. Go down to the water. Hurry.

I rush back down the bank, slipping, and hurry along the river edge, listening, listening, listening, but all I can hear is the crashing of the water.

I am so afraid that Phoebe has fallen into the river. I yell for her, but I cannot even hear myself over the churning water.

I go back and forth along the river edge, retracing my steps, over and over. Mama is saying the same thing, over and over: *Hurry, Charlie Anne, hurry.* I tell her to stop so I can listen. Is somebody moaning?

Yes, Mama tells me. *Yes, yes, yes. Hurry, Charlie Anne, hurry.*

My heart is leaping. I run, screaming "Phoebe, Phoebe," and right then and there I start praying to the angels again, because it's the only thing I can think of. Please, I pray. Please, please, please, let the best friend I ever had keep being the best friend I ever had.

And then I hear it, a tiny, thin little voice. Phoebe! I
look around me, all around, but there is nothing out of
place on the ridge, nothing on the bank, nothing along
the river. But I hear it again, and this time it is louder.
It is awfully sad and awfully tired and awfully hurt.

Hurry, Charlie Anne, hurry! screams Mama.

I rush toward the voice, a moaning coming from
behind a pine tree, and then I stop because there is my
Phoebe on the ground. Her face is turned up and she is
very still and worst of all, her foot is caught in one of
the Thatcher boys' rusty old traps. There's a big red *T*
painted on the side, and the rushing in my head starts
as soon as I see the blood, and I believe I am going to
fall over right here. "Oh," I say. "Oh, oh, oh."

She is wearing boots, but the trap has chewed right
through the rubber and there is blood coming out.
Then she is moaning again. I say a prayer to the angels
that I won't faint and fall over. "Phoebe, Phoebe. I am
here," I say, kneeling down.

She doesn't do anything but moan. Big moans, now,
and I am afraid, and I don't know what I should do. She
is lying on the ground and her skin is river cold.

"Phoebe. It is me. Charlie Anne."

Phoebe does nothing but moan a little more, and then she opens her eyes and closes them again. I take off my jacket and make a pillow for her and lift her head up real careful, and then I am not sure what to do. I put my head on her chest and listen to her heart. It is a slow quiet beat.

Her foot is a terrible-looking thing, and I try and pull the jaws of the trap apart, but they are strong. I pull at the chain that holds the trap to the tree, but I can't break it, and the moving makes Phoebe moan. I cry out to Mama. I am not sure if I should leave Phoebe or if I should stay. I am not sure if she will be alive when I come back.

I rush along the river, looking for a rock big enough to smash the chain, and Mama tells me that won't work, that I need something to wedge the trap open, but I tell her that maybe she doesn't know everything, and I carry a rock as big around as a slop bucket and drop it on the chain, and that makes Phoebe cry out and then faint.

Then I start sobbing.

Stand up, Charlie Anne. This is no time for quitting.

Mama says to go find a rock that is shaped more like a fence stake so I can wedge it in the trap and force it open. The trap is big and Phoebe's foot is small and it might work, says Mama.

Phoebe is moaning again. "I'll be right back," I whisper in her ear.

New tears are falling down my face and I have to wipe them away so I can see my way back down to the river.

I rush down the hill, searching along the river for a rock the right size. After about a hundred years, I find something at the edge of the water that might work, and I rush back to Phoebe.

I wedge the rock in the space between her foot and the side edge of the trap and push, and I scream out to Mama, and Phoebe lets out a terrible cry as the trap opens, and then she faints again.

"Phoebe!" I scream. "Now don't you go and die." Then I stagger quite a bit as I try and pick her up, and I slip, but I keep holding on to Phoebe, I keep holding on, and when I finally get her up into my arms, I tell my legs they better carry me and my best friend up the hill.

Good job, says Mama.

I am rushing, but Phoebe keeps sliding down from my arms, and I have to keep hoisting her back up, and when I do, she whimpers, and it cuts right through my heart. By the time I get out to the cornfield, I am nearly dropping her.

But there is Mirabel way down at the clothesline, hurrying to bring in all those wet sheets. I am glad to see her, even though she is probably good and mad at me right now, and I scream for her. She looks up, wondering why I am carrying such a big load.

"MIRABEL!"

It takes her only a moment to know there is something terribly wrong, and she throws the sheets on the ground and rushes toward me.

She has trouble running. She keeps hoisting her dress up over her knees. "Oh my God," she says when she sees the blood, and Mirabel is reaching for Phoebe and pulling her into her arms. She hugs Phoebe to her chest and rushes for Old Mr. Jolly's house and I am flying right behind.

At the door, I don't bother knocking, I fling it open, and there are Rosalyn and Old Mr. Jolly having a fight over some sort of paint job Rosalyn wants to do.

"She's real bad," I tell them, and Mirabel lays Phoebe on the couch and we all crowd around and Rosalyn starts to cry.

It turns out that Mirabel is good at big cuts, too, and she gently pulls the boot off Phoebe and I think I am going to faint from all the blood and Mirabel tells Rosalyn to help her prop up Phoebe's feet and then go and get a washbucket and lots of cloths, and while Mirabel is getting the bleeding to stop, Rosalyn sponges off Phoebe's face and I hold her hand. Phoebe cries out and Mirabel asks Rosalyn to soothe her and sing to her and try and keep her quiet and I thank Mama that Mirabel is getting everything right.

Old Mr. Jolly is already in his coat and hat. There is no hospital for one hundred miles, but there is a doctor, three towns over. Old Mr. Jolly comes over and lays his hand on Phoebe's face and then reaches out and squeezes Rosalyn's hand, and she tells him how scared she is and he says, "Me too," and then he says, "Take care of our little girl."

And then he is gone and I am all choked up and we are left with Mirabel telling us how making sure the wound is clean is the most important thing. Mirabel makes me keep getting fresh water from the well, and as I do, I am thinking about how sorry I am about everything, about my terrible bad behavior when Phoebe was my teacher assistant and my awful manners and how I'd like to take everything back.

Phoebe falls asleep and Mirabel says this is the best thing and then Birdie and Ivy are coming in and Birdie is climbing all over me and she is crying because she doesn't understand things like sometimes you can get caught in a trap and you can't get out, unless someone is there to help you.

After about a thousand years, Old Mr. Jolly comes back with the doctor. I see a surprised look on the doctor's face when he sees Phoebe. He is in an awful hurry and I wonder about that and he tells us how we haven't done anything right and how Phoebe shouldn't be sleeping and she shouldn't have her foot up so high and I am feeling like Mirabel has been telling us to do all the wrong things.

Then he looks at her foot again and bandages it up and puts her foot as high as Mirabel had it and gives Rosalyn some medicine that will help Phoebe sleep and he stands up to leave and Rosalyn asks if Phoebe will be all right and the doctor says he thinks so but only time will tell.

Well. That's not very helpful, I think. He and Old Mr. Jolly are walking out to the porch and Old Mr. Jolly is reaching in his pocket and giving the doctor money and explaining how he is sorry there isn't more to give and I want to know for sure, is Phoebe going to be all right, and so I follow them.

"You know, Jolly, if I'd have known . . . ," the doctor is saying, putting the money in his pocket.

"Known what?" Old Mr. Jolly is asking.

"You know what I'm saying without me having to say it," the doctor says.

"In case I don't," says Old Mr. Jolly, his voice hard, "why don't you go ahead and say it?"

"All right, I will." The doctor puts on his hat. "I've got patients stacked ten high back at the house, all of them with influenza. And none of them are colored." Then the doctor finishes buttoning his coat and puts on his hat and walks out.

I can hardly believe the terrible thing the doctor just said. Old Mr. Jolly stands there on the porch, looking at me. Then he hurries down the porch stairs, his shoulders all hunched, his face red. He picks up a rock from the driveway and stands there, tossing the stone in his hands. Then he winds up, aiming straight at the doctor's car. I hold my breath, hoping the rock will smash a window.

I am getting all light-headed from holding my breath so long and watching Old Mr. Jolly just winding up. And then, very slowly he puts his hand down, and then he drops the rock on the driveway and he turns and walks up on the porch. "He's not worth it," he says when he sees me.

Then Old Mr. Jolly smiles a sad smile, and I follow him inside and notice how tall he walks now. I'm not going to be able to call him Old Mr. Jolly anymore.

* * *

Right away, as soon as Phoebe starts resting peacefully and Mirabel tells us it is time to go, I have to go right up and tell Mama about the whole awful day.

It was terrible. I thought Phoebe was going to die. I thought I was going to faint with all the blood.

But you didn't, Mama says.

No. I'm pretty mad at that Thatcher boy for leaving that trap there.

Yes. It is very sad.

Mama, the doctor said awful things.

I know. I heard it, too. What are you going to do?

Me?

Mama laughs gently. *I know you, Charlie Anne. I saw you get Belle home, remember? You have to show people like that doctor that they are wrong.*

How?

You'll find a way. Then Mama pauses. *You could become a doctor yourself.*

Don't you have to read to be a doctor?

Mmmmmm, says Mama. *But you'll be surprised how things can change. Just give it a little more time.*

I'm also very afraid of blood.

Is that so? Mama says, and then she starts laughing so hard that pretty soon I am laughing, too. It is a pretty nice change to a terrible day.

Two very good things happen after that, which makes the bad thing that happens not as bad as it could be. Life is like that, if you look hard enough. The good will outweigh the bad if you give it half a chance.

The first good thing is Phoebe starts healing. It is slow going at first. I go check up on her every day and sit on the chair and watch her lying all still in her bed. Each day I bring a bouquet of dried goldenrod or Queen Anne's lace and put it on her nightstand. At first, I can't tell if she even knows I'm there, and so I spend the whole time telling her, "Hi, Phoebe, it's me, Charlie Anne," and praying to the angels that I will get my friend back.

Then she stops sleeping so much, and her foot must hurt more than anything because she gets really grouchy and she cries a lot. Then as she gets even better, she gets so bossy I don't even want to be near her. "The sun is in my eyes, can't you move the curtain right?" she says, and then "Charlie Anne, go get me some sweet raspberry tea," and "Charlie Anne, it's not sweet enough," and "Charlie Anne, you didn't put enough raspberries in."

Mirabel says this grouchiness is to be expected, and

that brings me to the other good thing that happens. Mirabel says Ivy can do more of my chores now so I can come over and be with Phoebe.

I try to figure it out, when did Mirabel change her mind about Phoebe? I guess it happened when Mirabel picked up Phoebe in her arms and carried her, and she saw how carrying her was just like carrying any other child. In fact, she keeps sending me over to check on Phoebe, and usually she sends me with some kind of potato casserole she has made. And then she comes over in the afternoon and helps Rosalyn take off the bandage and soak Phoebe's foot and wraps it up again. There has been a lot of foot washing around here.

Ivy is very mad about all of this.

"Mind your manners," Mirabel tells her.

The bad thing that happens is Rosalyn tells me we won't be opening the school, not for a long while. Mr. Jolly and I have to go tell the Morrell girls, and when we do, Sarah starts to cry.

One day, when I am trying to get the temperature of Phoebe's tea just right, Rosalyn starts drawing pictures on little pieces of paper and cutting out letters and putting everything in a big basket.

"How would you like to try this again?" Rosalyn wants to know.

I look up at Phoebe.

"She's fallen asleep," whispers Rosalyn. "We have time."

She draws a picture.

"What's this?" she asks.

"Hen," I say.

Rosalyn studies it. "Well, it's really a duck, but hen is all right. Here, I'll draw another one."

"Turkey," I say.

After that, Rosalyn gives me the pen and tells me to draw the pictures.

This is something I am good at. She tells me to draw a house, and I do, and Rosalyn says, "Wow, Charlie Anne, you are really good at drawing," and then she tells me to draw a baby and then a door and then a barn and then a clothesline. I am very good at drawing all of these things. Pretty soon we have a whole stack of little pictures. We put them in the basket.

"Now, let's cut out some letters."

Rosalyn helps me draw the alphabet and then we cut everything out. Then we go check on Phoebe, who is still sleeping, and Rosalyn makes a cup of sweet raspberry tea for each of us and gives me a strawberry tart she has been saving for me. "Reading takes a lot of energy, Charlie Anne." I tell her between bites that I think she's right, and then she tells me to close my eyes and pick out six of the pictures, and then we spread them out on the table.

Rosalyn spreads all the letters on the table, and she asks me to say the word for the picture on the first paper.

"Door," I say.

"What sound does *door* make? Sound it out."

"*D-d-d-d.*"

"Very good. What letter is that, *d-d-d?*"

I look at all the letters that are lying on the table. I know it is a *d-d-d-d* sound, and I know that sound is made by either a *b* or a *d*.

I am afraid of making a mistake, so I sit on my hands and think about it for a while longer.

Don't be afraid, Mama says. *Everyone makes mistakes when they are learning something new. Rosalyn will understand.*

Then I make a fist and stick my thumb up, just like Rosalyn taught me. I look at Rosalyn and try and imagine what she will do if I say the wrong thing. I think about Miss Moran and that spot under her desk where I had to sit and how there was a spiderweb way in the back corner.

I look back at the letters. They are looking all jumbled up and pushed together and I can't remember what anything says anymore and I am starting to feel very, very hot.

Rosalyn is looking at me. "It's hard, isn't it?" she says gently. "Reading is hard at the beginning. But I have an idea. Let's spend more time on the letters first, before we start on the pictures. Let's talk for a long time about each letter and about what each letter says and about what sound each letter makes."

So we start at the beginning, the very beginning, because just like a house, reading needs a good foundation.

I lay all the letters on the table and we look at them and make the sound of each one. We spend a very long time on the *b*s and the *d*s. I make another *bed* with my letters.

When Rosalyn thinks I may understand the difference, she points to the picture of the door again.

"What is it, a *b* or a *d*?"

Right then and there, I feel a smile start spreading across my face, and then I am laughing out loud.

"It's a *d*."

Day after day, Rosalyn tells me what pictures to draw and I draw them and then I tell her what letter they start with. I have about a hundred little pictures. Mr. Jolly props Phoebe up on the couch so she can be closer to us.

"You should play I Spy with Charlie Anne, like you and Mama did with me when I was learning," Phoebe says.

And so that's what we do next. Only, Rosalyn makes Phoebe teach me. This is good for Phoebe because she has to sit up, and we spread all the pictures out on her lap, and she says, "I see something that starts with *t*." Then I have to spend about a hundred years looking for something that starts with *t*. Phoebe doesn't want me to miss anything.

Finally, when Phoebe thinks I have looked long and hard enough, she says, "Well?" and I pick up a turtle, a trumpet and a pair of trousers.

One day the three Morrell girls and their mama come to visit Phoebe with a pint of blackberry jam and some fresh biscuits, and when they see us playing I Spy, they ask if they can play, and Rosalyn says of course.

"Sit here," I say, spreading the drawings all over Phoebe.

"I spy some things that begin with *m*," says Phoebe. "Can you find them, Charlie Anne?"

It doesn't take me long to find the mouse, the mitten and the manger. Then it's my turn. "Sarah," I say, "I spy some things that begin with *s*." She finds the bag of sugar, the saw and the strawberry.

She turns to her sister. "Mary, I spy some things that begin with *p*."

While we are playing, Rosalyn is brewing up some sweet raspberry tea. By the way the Morrell girls smack their lips, I think sweet raspberry tea is something they haven't had in a while.

Then Rosalyn asks Mrs. Morrell how they are all

getting along, and Mrs. Morrell says they are doing much better now that she is over the influenza. "Mirabel has been coming over and helping out some days. She's going to the Thatchers' after she leaves me. I hear the influenza is finally out of their house, too."

"Maybe we should open the school right here in our living room while Phoebe is healing," Rosalyn says one day.

She says I have to invite Ivy and of course Birdie wants to come. "Go invite Becky Ellis again," she tells me. "People have a way of changing."

Well. I hope not. I stall for three days and Rosalyn keeps asking if I've been over to see Becky. Finally, I go knock on their door.

"Rosalyn wants to know if you'll send Becky to school at her house, while Phoebe is recuperating."

"I think not," says Mrs. Ellis, without inviting me in.

It takes a few more days, but good manners finally get the better of Mrs. Ellis. She and Becky call on us and ask about Phoebe. Mrs. Ellis brings a lemon tart, and Rosalyn cuts it into neat slices.

"Why, it's such a beautiful tart," says Rosalyn, smiling brightly.

"Thank you," says Mrs. Ellis, sipping on sweet raspberry tea.

Then Rosalyn says maybe Becky might want to come to our school and help teach reading, seeing as she's so advanced and all. "She's at the top of the class."

"Well," says Mrs. Ellis, sipping at her tea. "Maybe. Maybe she will."

CHAPTER

48

We start thinking about doing that play again, and I tell everyone I am not being the donkey, no matter what.

Since no one else wants to be stage director, I volunteer for the job. This means I get to make decisions about everything. It turns out I am very good at this.

And so on the day that Becky starts coming to our school in Phoebe's living room, I tell her she has to be the donkey this year. Right away she starts screaming, and it takes a long time for me to tell her I was only kidding and that we're not going to even have a donkey this year.

"You can be an angel, Becky. And Sarah and Deborah and Mary get to be angels, too."

"But I am the only one with wings."

"We can sew, Becky," I say, pointing to my new poppy-colored trousers and eyeing the basket of fabric on the table.

"I noticed," she says, looking at my trousers, then over at Ivy, and rolling her eyes.

Birdie comes over and tells me she doesn't want to be an angel, she wants to be a lemon-drop fairy.

Becky stomps her foot. "We don't have lemon-drop fairies in a Christmas play."

"Yes, we do," I tell her, picking up a piece of yellow fabric from the box. "Things are different now."

> Dear Papa,
>   We are having our Christmas play and it won't be the same without you. Please come home. And bring Peter back from Aunt Eleanor's. And bring lemon drops for Birdie.
>   Love from your daughter,
>   Charlie Anne

"Good job," says Phoebe, who has been helping me with what I want to say.

Then I decide to write out invitations for everyone else in town, everyone except the Thatchers. Mr. Jolly says that's okay. He's not ready for the Thatchers, either.

Phoebe helps me write on the invitations that everyone should come with a candle, and when we light them, we will be one light.

And wouldn't you know it? At five o'clock I see half our town coming up the walk of our little church. Mr. Jolly carries Phoebe in, and there is a lot of whispering about how maybe she is going to sing again.

"Did you know she has the voice of an angel?" Mrs. Aldrich is telling her daughter, who is visiting with five little grandchildren.

I hear Mirabel telling Zella that Phoebe is the Jollys' new daughter. "I'm surprised you didn't know that," she says, and I smile to myself.

Since I let everyone who wanted to be an angel get to be one, we have four of them, plus a lemon-drop fairy. Rosalyn made all the wings, and now Birdie and the Morrell girls have wings as beautiful as the ones that Becky Ellis is wearing. Mrs. Morrell dabs at her eyes as she watches her little girls glitter in the candlelight.

I am so happy to see them sparkling that I think maybe I'm going straight to heaven at this very minute to be with Mama. But I don't. It is time for the play, and it is time for the heavenly chorus, which is the part we made special, just for Phoebe. Mr. Jolly carries her up front and she leans against him. I nod and smile at her, and then the organ starts and Phoebe opens her mouth, and just like that, heaven comes out:

Bright morning stars are rising,
Bright morning stars are rising,
Bright morning stars are rising,
Day is a-breaking in my soul.

I look over at Mr. and Mrs. Aldrich and notice they have tears in their eyes.

*   *   *

The moon is full and the stars are filling up the heavens and I tell Mama as I walk home that the only thing missing from tonight is my family, still all broken apart.

49

"All right, everyone. Make your manners."

This is how Rosalyn starts the day, now that we have opened the little schoolhouse again. I think she sounds a little like Mirabel. But Rosalyn says if we are respectful of each other, things will go better for all of us.

"Good morning, Charlie Anne." This is my cue to stand up beside my desk, which I do.

"Good morning, Rosalyn."

"My, those are lovely trousers. They remind me of the violets growing along your stone wall."

I am beaming. "Mirabel and I made them out of one of her old dresses." I turn this way and then that beside my desk, and the rest of the class is wanting a pair, I can tell.

"How's your reading coming along, Charlie Anne?"

"Much better," I say.

"Would you show me in a bit?"

I grin. "I am ready," I tell her.

She moves to the next desk.

"Good morning, Phoebe."

"Good morning, Rosalyn."

* * *

It was Mr. Jolly's idea to get Mrs. Thatcher to send her oldest boy up north to build roads. "He needs to get out and see how the world works," he told her, and she went along with the idea, as long as Mr. Jolly promised to help her other boys with the heavy work. He's got those boys fixing the porch and chopping wood and getting the barn ready for a cow in the spring. "Charlie Anne will help you pick one," he told Mrs. Thatcher, winking at me. "She's very good with cows, you know."

The rest of the Thatcher boys seem to be taking to school pretty well. They all have runny noses. Perhaps the golden harvest soup that is bubbling on the woodstove by Rosalyn's desk will take care of that.

Looking at the Thatcher boys makes me miss Peter and feel all the broken Peter-places still in my heart.

Rosalyn calls me up to her desk. She places *First Reader* in my hands.

"Let's try some of these words."

I look at the list, at all the *b*s and all the *d*s, and I think about Miss Moran and the awful place under her desk.

"Come on, Charlie Anne," says Rosalyn all softlike. "It's just like I Spy. Don't quit."

I notice her brown eyes. They are almost as nice as Anna May's. I look at the first word. I hold up my left hand and make a fist. "B . . . a . . . ll, d . . . o . . . ll, d . . . e . . . ll."

"My heavens, you're a wonderful reader," says Rosalyn. Then she picks up *Second Reader* and places it in my hands. "I think you're ready for this."

I am? Me? Charlie Anne?

Yes, Mama whispers. *You are.*

I look at the words, and they jumble up. But I take a deep breath and tell them to stop, and wouldn't you know it, they start minding their manners.

I hold up my left hand again and make another fist. Then I take a breath. "A . . . b-i-rd . . . b-u-i-lt . . . its . . . n-e-st," I read. I peek over the top of the book because I can't help myself. I want to see Rosalyn's face.

She is leaning forward, holding her breath.

"In the n-e-st were f-our wh-ite e-ggs, with . . ." I stop again to see if it's a *b* or a *d.* "Br-ow-n sp-ecks."

"Yes," Rosalyn says softly, "that's it, Charlie Anne. I knew you could. Now, keep going."

And then I am all fired up. "O-u-t of th-ese f-our eggs ca-me four wee b-i-rds. Their sk-in was b-a-re, and they could not fly; b-u-t the old birds ke-pt them wa-rm."

And then I peek over the top of my book and see what I have never seen before. Rosalyn is sitting there with big tears falling down her face. And they are for me.

"I knew you could, Charlie Anne."

5 0

Mirabel tells me I have to go get the clothes off the line. More snow's coming, she tells me, and I tell her, "Well, why the dickens didn't you think about this when I was out there hanging it all up?" Even Belle and Anna May want to know.

She puts her hands on her hips and asks me if I need to start reading that book again. I tell her no. "No, I do not."

Then she says that when I am out by the clothesline, maybe I could walk down by the garden and see if there might be room for an extra two rows of peas in front of where we plant the corn. She wants me to measure it out with my feet. She is reading a book called *American Husbandry* and she wants me to read it, too. It is filled with ideas on how to run a farm even better, which pretty much means more chores for everybody. I tell her we don't need to be thinking about planting peas. We will be lucky to just get through all this snow.

She tells me not to worry about a little snow. She says I am strong as an ox.

Humph, I tell her. My boots are warming beside the cookstove. Mirabel says I should keep them there now because I have so many outside chores. I cut new pieces of cardboard because the holes in my boots are bigger than ever. I hunt through the rag basket for some extra wool to wrap around my feet, and I see that Mirabel has cut up Peter's old jacket and is making it smaller so Birdie can wear it.

Then I go outside. The snow is so cold it crunches under my feet like soda crackers. I start pulling the laundry off the line. What is Mirabel thinking? These blankets are wet and heavy and stiff as a barn door. I can hardly move under the weight of all the wool.

It is then that I hear a motor and I look at Belle and Anna May out by the butternut tree and they look up, wondering what all the noise is on this still day. Then a big black automobile comes driving up on our yard and hanging out the window is Peter and before the car even comes to a stop he is opening up the door and jumping out and running out to where I am running to him.

I drop the blankets and I don't care because there is Peter rushing toward me with his arms stretched out and then he is jumping up in my arms and I am falling down and hugging him and laughing, right there in the snow, and then Birdie is running out of the house and climbing on top of us and then wouldn't you know it, there is Ivy saying, "Peter, you're getting that fancy coat all wet," and sounding just like Mirabel.

Only, Mirabel isn't saying that. She is rushing off the porch toward us. She pulls Peter up off the ground, and then she holds his little face in her hands and smiles, and then she hugs him. She whispers to him, and I can't hear what she says, but I can imagine because when she stops squeezing him, she has tears in her eyes.

"I'm staying," he says, turning to the rest of us. "I'm staying home."

It isn't until a few minutes later, when we all head back to the house, that I overhear Aunt Eleanor telling Mirabel, "You should have told me he wet the bed like that. I've never seen anything like it. Poor Betty can't keep up with all the washing. And he cries every single night of the week. There's no stopping him."

I look across to Anna May and Belle. Their eyes are filled with cow-joy. It is a beautiful thing.

5 I

"This is how you milk a cow," I am telling Phoebe. "You have to stay away from her kicking foot, though."

We do this every morning together, now that March has come and the sun is trying to turn everything to spring. Phoebe is just terrible at milking Anna May. She can never get the milk started. When she gets a little trickle, she squirts in all the wrong directions, and now Little Peach Fuzz knows to come running and wait for all of Phoebe's mistakes.

"Well, will you look at that cow!" It's that voice—that deep, deep voice—that I haven't heard for a long, long time, and I don't need to turn around to know who it is.

"Papa!" I screech, and then I am flying up into his arms, and there is my brother Thomas, rubbing his chin, asking for something to eat.

"Any of that vinegar pie left around here?" Papa wants to know, and then he asks me other things, like who is my new friend, and I say, "Papa, this is Phoebe," and "Phoebe, this is Papa." Then I hug him some more and I bury my face in his neck and smell the soap he uses for shaving, and after a very long time, he pulls out a whole bag of lemon drops, and we hurry to the house because he wants to see Peter and everybody else. As we are all hugging and Birdie is jumping up in his arms, we make room for Phoebe, and then I am laughing out loud.

I have thought about this moment for a very long time, and I am glad it is just the way I wanted it to be.

Papa has a talk with Mr. Jolly. They decide we can keep Belle in our fields as long as I milk her twice a day and give Mr. Jolly half the milk.

"She's his cow, Charlie Anne."

"But we don't even milk her yet," I say, my cheeks puffed out with vinegar pie.

"Well, we're going to have to turn her into a milk cow, get her to give us a calf. I never heard of anyone waiting this long."

Another baby calf! My heart splits right there at the table, just like an old melon. But two seconds later I am thinking about new babies and mamas going straight to heaven and I am shaking my head.

"She'll be fine, Charlie Anne. She's fit as a fiddle. You've been taking fine care of her."

I send a little prayer to the angels, just to be sure. I tell them thank you for watching over us even when we are mad about things. Prayers are powerful things.

52

I feel a little terrible that I haven't been spending as much time with Mama. I have been reading so much and being with Phoebe and working on a new play for next Christmas, and I haven't been going up to see her. So one day when the sun is out, I put on my new coat and new boots that Papa brought home and go up and find a warm spot where the sun is beating down, and it feels almost like spring.

Papa's home, I tell her.

Mama smiles her warm happy smile that spreads all over me. *I know, Charlie Anne. He's been out to see me.*

I missed him so much.

I know, she tells me, pulling me close.

I don't want him to go away again.

Did you tell him that?

Yes. But he keeps saying there's more than one way to keep a family together, and if it gets bad again, he may have to go, but he'll try not to.

I lean back. Papa says Mirabel can stay, too, because we need her. I told him I don't want her to be our new mama, and he said he doesn't like her like that anyway.

This makes Mama laugh. Then she notices my boots.

I wiggle them out in front of me. I don't have to put rags in to make them fit, I tell her.

I see, says Mama.

After a while, I am so happy and warm being close to Mama and with the sun beating down that I start feeling a little sleepy. I've been reading, I tell her as I start closing my eyes.

Mmmmmm, says Mama. *I've been listening.*

Sometimes you really do get what you hope for, don't you?

Mmmmmm, says Mama, pulling me closer. *Sometimes you do.*

ACKNOWLEDGMENTS

With sincere gratitude, I thank my readers for their insight and encouragement: my parents, the Still River Writers, elementary and special-needs teacher (and fellow writer) Laurie Smith Murphy, and folk musicians Aubrey Atwater and Elwood Donnelly, who also contributed their knowledge of traditional music and song.

Thank you also to my research help: retired elementary school teacher Beverly Pettine for introducing me to the Hornbine one-room schoolhouse, a living-history museum in Rehoboth, Massachusetts, where she teaches, for sharing primers used during the Great Depression, for reading the manuscript, and for also introducing me to Evelyn Rose Bois and Frances Magan Jones, who attended the school during the 1920s and 1930s. I thank these women for their humor and keen memories, and for sharing the trash-bucket, under-the-desk, and woodshed punishments (which went to the boys, not to them).

Thank you to Elizabeth Stevens Brown, 1879–1941, an African American woman and daughter of a coachman, who began teaching in a Swansea, Massachusetts, wooden schoolhouse in 1901 and who became a beloved principal in that town in 1932. Her students remember her writing the "Whatever you are, be noble" poem on her blackboard each morning.

I am indebted to Janette Huling, 4-H Dairy Club leader in Exeter, Rhode Island, for introducing me to her Holstein and Brown Swiss dairy cows and for answering all my questions. Although I spent many hours as a child around cows on family farms in Maine, I needed a refresher course.

I am thankful for Helen Ekin Starrett's *The Charm of Fine Manners*, published in 1907. There is much in the book that Charlie Anne rebels against, but there is much that still shines. As Charlie Anne learns to read, she becomes able to evaluate information and ideas and can decide for herself what parts of a book to accept and believe and what parts to ignore.

I thank my agent, Elizabeth Harding, vice president of Curtis Brown Ltd., for her encouragement, and my editor, Michelle Frey, executive editor of Knopf Books for Young Readers, for her talent and for believing in me and in this novel.

Finally, I thank my husband for his encouragement and assistance throughout the many months of writing, and for reading *The Wonder of Charlie Anne* over and over again.